I0452358

Running on Empty

Bon Chance Boonies, Volume 1

A. L. Vincent

Published by Bienvenue Press, 2021.

This one is dedicated to two badass women in my life. Zelda and Colleen D. This one's for you two. "Here's to Us."

Acknowledgements

First of all, special thanks to some of my favorite local musicians. Neil, Baret, Nick, and Joey, thanks for all the great music and memories. Many more to come!

Thanks to Gillian, Dennis, and Steve for the editing jobs you guys do.

Also, I have to give nods to my "Boonies." Ruby, Melinda, Tammy, Val, Denise, Sandy, Stacey, and Elizabeth, thank you for all of your support throughout the writing and publishing process.

Much love and many thanks to you all. You guys rock!

Chapter One

Grace Delchamp stood center stage. Head lowered, she stared at the yellow wires taped to the stage through a veil of black hair. The spotlight focused on her, its heat magnifying the sultry air wafting in from the open doors of the Bourbon Street bar.

Brent Mouton, the band's lead guitarist and other singer, played the first few bars of their signature song. Grace lifted her head and began to sing. The first part of the song was acoustic—her vocals that some had called "haunting" rang through the crowd accompanied only by the sound of Brent's guitar.

Her voice rose with the chorus. As she sang, the crowd melted away, along with any residual nervousness. It was simply her and the melody. Nothing else.

Grace lived for that moment. The crowd didn't matter. The applause didn't matter. For her, this was it. She thrived on it, ate it up, and gave it everything she had.

Her voice trailed off as the song ended. She grinned and nodded as the crowd applauded. The next song on the set list was a fast one, a hard rocking song from the '80s. Grace threw her hair back and played with the audience, making eye contact with the obviously single guys and winking, getting the girls in the bachelorette parties to sing along on the mic.

When everyone joined in, Grace knew they were all having a good time.

Song after song, the show continued, until Grace was slick with sweat and euphoria. Adrenaline coursed through her, firing her up even more.

She and Brent belted out the last few bars of the Def Leppard hit *Pour Some Sugar on Me* and then it was break time. She walked off the stage, white towel in hand, to the bar. She needed something cold to drink.

She held the towel to her neck with one hand while she sipped the drink with the other. Feeling a presence lurking behind her, she turned, one eyebrow raised, ready to let a drunk tourist have it.

Seeing her older brother and his best friend's smiling faces behind her, she shouted, "Joey! Carly!"

"You surprised?" Joey asked. His dark hair was, as always, slightly disheveled. Usually in t-shirts with off-the-wall sayings, tonight he had chosen to wear a Saints monogrammed pullover and khaki shorts.

"Yes!"

"Carly won ghost tour tickets in a writing contest, so we all came up."

"I'm so excited!" Carly said. "And we're staying at the Chateau Rouge again! I hope I see a ghost this time!"

Carly had also dressed up for the night out. Her blonde hair, usually in a ponytail, floated around her shoulders. She wore a cute, flowered sundress. She was often compared to Drew Barrymore, and tonight Grace could see the resemblance.

"Come on," Joey said, tucking his hand under her elbow. "Em and Noah are here. Come meet us!"

Grace followed Joey and Carly to the courtyard area away from the crowd. For Noah, Grace knew. Noah, an Iraq war veteran, still had issues that would probably never go away. Dealing with crowds was one. The fact that he was in New Orleans on Bourbon Street on a weekend was a testament to how much he had changed since he and Emily had been together. Emily's quiet and calm presence probably had a lot to do with those changes. Emily had recently followed her dream and opened the Bon Chance Catering Company. She was now traveling all over southern Louisiana setting up jobs. Noah had chosen to work with his hands in solitude. He ran his own construction company. In Grace's opinion, the two could not be more perfect for each other.

One summer years ago, Carly, the imaginative one, had christened the group "The Boonies". The Boonies was loosely based on an '80s movie that had sent them all on a search for Jean Lafitte's treasure. That, and the fact that in their teens they had considered the small coastal town of Bon Chance to be in the boondocks. It was far removed from all the action in the big cities of New Orleans, Baton Rouge, or Biloxi.

Emily and Noah were the oldest of the group. Carly and Joey were next in age. Carly was Noah's younger sister, and Joey was Grace's older brother. Carly, Joey, and Noah had gone into business together the year before, opening Snapper's Bar and Grill.

The youngest and biggest group was Grace's circle. It consisted of Grace, Ryder, Gabriel, and Benjamin. Benjamin, Carly and Noah's younger brother, had passed away a few years ago in an oil rig accident.

"I see your friends are here," Brent said, walking up behind Grace.

Grace stiffened and resisted the urge to roll her eyes. Things with Brent and her had become tense lately. He kept asking her out for dinner, for drinks, for sex—all which Grace kept refusing. The man was much too self-absorbed and arrogant for her taste. Grace could see the train wreck that getting involved with him would be from a mile away. Brent had grown up in Pointe Shade, a small town just down the road from Bon Chance. He was a Mouton, and that meant trouble. His uncle thought he owned the town, and probably did own most of it. As a result, his kinfolk thought everything else belonged to them too. Even women.

"Yes, Brent."

"We're here for a ghost tour and Bourbon Street, of course," Carly chimed in, always ready for a party. Brent's eyes shifted to the blond beauty.

Oh Lord, Grace thought, *here we go.*

"Well, hello, Carly. You look amazing tonight as usual."

Grace cut her eyes to Joey, who was frowning. But then again, so was Noah. But Carly could handle herself.

"And don't you look...sweaty," Carly said, smiling with a wrinkle of her nose. It was a jab, and Grace resisted the urge to laugh.

Brent frowned, his blue eyes narrowed. He turned to Grace. "Well, we're back up in five minutes."

"I'll be there."

Brent disappeared back through the crowd in the bar.

"What was that all about?" Carly asked as soon as he was gone.

"Oh, he's being an ass. He gets more conceited every day. He thinks he's God's gift to women. And doesn't like taking no for an answer. No matter how many times you turn him down. It's getting aggravating."

Carly shook her head. "Men!"

"It's nothing I can't handle," Grace said, downing her drink as she looked at her phone. "Well, guys, it's time for me to get back up there. I'll see y'all soon," she said, hugging them. "Have fun!"

Chapter Two

G race woke up to the alarm buzzing on the nightstand. Feeling lightheaded, she blinked in confusion. Her eyes widened when she realized she wasn't alone. Who was in bed with her? She glanced over to see Brent lying beside her.

She sat up in bed, shaking her head and blinking. Her head felt like it was full of cotton. Looking down, she realized her state of undress. She grabbed the sheet and covered herself. Her head swam with the unfamiliar dizziness. This was not what drunk felt like. She took deep breaths to keep from vomiting as her stomach heaved in turmoil.

What happened?

"What did you do?" Grace whispered to Brent, fearing the answer.

"You don't remember?" Brent asked, smiling.

Grace scanned her memory. The band had gone for a few drinks after practice. Later, only Grace and Brent remained. They had toasted to a good show. They'd listened to a few songs and made a little small talk about new music selections. That was it. How had she gotten back to her apartment? She closed her eyes, trying to remember.

Nothing.

Had she walked?

Nothing.

Her heart began racing. What had she done? Her mind was hazy, the memories shrouded like a curtain.

"What did we do?"

He climbed out of bed and started pulling on clothes.

"Brent! I never would have slept with you. I told you no repeatedly. What did you do?"

"I'll never tell," he said. "Bye, sweetheart. It was fun."

Grace searched her memory again, the fear chasing the fog from her mind. She remembered drinks, the round of shots Brent had brought back from the bar. The shots. That was the last thing she recalled.

"You put something in my drink, didn't you?"

"Does it matter now?" he asked. Now clothed, he walked toward the bedroom door.

"This isn't over," she whispered as another wave of nausea rolled through her stomach. "I will make sure you pay for this."

"What are you going to do? Who's going to believe you? And don't forget Sheriff Mouton is my dear uncle. I won't pay for anything. Where do you think the stuff came from?"

Grace grabbed one of her high-heeled black leather boots off the floor beside the bed and threw it across the small room.

"You aren't going to do anything. I'll see you tonight at the show." And he walked out the door.

Grace's heart pounded as she stared at the closed door. Adrenaline pushed away the nausea and the fog. Looking down, she saw the match to the black boot she had thrown at Brent. She picked it up and threw it at the door.

"I'm not going to do anything?" she yelled at the door. "Watch me."

Grace jumped out of bed and grabbed some clothes out of her dresser. Looking at them, folded and clean, she shuddered. She couldn't put them on yet. Not without showering. She stalked into the bathroom and turned the water on the hottest temperature. When she was finally convinced she had scrubbed all remnants of the encounter away, she stepped out and toweled off.

Still in a towel, she went back in the bedroom. She saw the rumpled bed. She strode over to it and grabbed the black sheets. With a tug, she pulled everything off the bed, throwing it into a pile in the far corner of the room. When that was done, she stomped on them. Once. Then twice.

Her lips curled in a sneer. She took one last glance at the sheets and turned to get her travel bag.

"See me tonight? I don't think so, Brent."

Then, in a whisper, "And yes. I will see that you pay for this. Somehow."

She tossed a few changes of clothes and toiletries in the bag, threw it over her shoulder with her guitar, and walked out the door.

· · · ·

EMPTY.

On the side of the quiet highway, Grace kicked the motorcycle and cursed. The gas tank was empty. . The gas gauge had been acting up for weeks and Grace hadn't had the chance to take it in. In the chaos after waking up with Brent, she hadn't topped it off with fuel.

She had only three miles to go and she'd be home in the little town of Bon Chance on the Louisiana coast. Three miles to the safety of her childhood home, best friends, and family.

She glanced at her phone. She should call Joey or Ryder and have them come get her rather than walk on a mostly deserted highway. Asking for help had never come easily. Three miles would not be a long stretch. She expended more energy than that performing with the band on stage or on a morning run along the canal. Besides, the exercise would be welcome. She palmed the pepper spray hanging from her keychain and thought of the knife in her boot. God help the man who chose to mess with her today.

Grace pulled off the motorcycle helmet and felt the long braid fall against her back. She threw her guitar case and travel bag over one shoulder. She unzipped the kennel bungee corded securely to the passenger's seat and took out the small white and brown dog of indiscernible breed and nuzzled him to her face. His white fur contrasted with the wisps of black hair that had escaped and fell across her face.

She had rescued the dog as a puppy. She had found him eating out of a dumpster behind a bar on Bourbon. A small, dirty ball of matted hair, she brought him home, bathed and fed him. She named him Furball, or Furby, for short.

She placed Furby back in the kennel, cradling it to her chest. He squirmed until she unzipped the top so he could poke his head out.

As she walked alone down the old highway, Grace let herself be comforted by the familiar sights and the warmth of the sun on her face. She passed the old cemetery with its white tombs jutting up, casting shadows on the grass.

When she passed the kayak and boat rental store, she knew that soon, the Gulf would be in view. She could already hear the seagulls calling. It was sweet music calling her home. Slowly, the town she loved came into view. She passed the open-air market where farmers displayed their produce. Familiar faces smiled as she waved. She walked by the one grocery/convenience/gas station where everyone went for coffee and the day's gossip. Snapper's Bar and Grill was next. She would stop by later to have a drink and visit with the regulars. She would also text Ryder. Maybe a few drinks with him and a few spins around the dance floor would help her regain a sense of security.

Not far from Snapper's was Joey's house. It was the classic coastal camp elevated on stilts and slightly weathered grey from the salty air and wind. Their parents had left it to them when they had retired and moved to the Florida coast with Carly and Noah's parents. Her brother's shiny black Jeep and boat were nestled underneath. He wouldn't go into the bar to cook until later. She walked up the steps and crept quietly to her former bedroom, relishing the familiarity. The same rock posters hung over the bed as when she was younger. The same blanket laid on the bed, the same pictures of friends and family were on the dresser.

"Look, Furby. It's my old room." She let him down and he ran around sniffing everything while she took off her boots and got undressed.

Exhausted and feeling dirty from the road but too tired to shower, she dropped the beat-up leather traveling bag and guitar case on the floor by the bed. Furby, having found everything to his satisfaction, jumped up on the pillow beside her head and they slept.

• • • •

GRACE JUMPED WHEN A hand touched her shoulder. Heart racing, her eyes popped open. She saw her brother's face. Her fears were chased away by her brother's dimpled smile.

"Grace? What are you doing here?" He stepped back from the bed, and she could see his rumpled dark hair in the light from the open doorway. He wore the Saints pajama pants she had bought him for Christmas and a battered t-shirt that had once bore a witty saying but had faded to something indiscriminate.

"I needed a place to think," she said. She could not tell Joey what happened with Brent.

"You okay?"

Unable to lie to him, she said, "Not really."

"What can I do to help?"

Needing to change the subject, Grace told him about the bike. "Can I borrow your truck to go get it?"

"Don't be silly. I'll go grab Noah and we'll get it. Don't worry about anything, get some rest. You look like hell. Come to Snapper's later and I'll cook you some lunch."

"Sounds good."

He ruffled her hair like he'd done so many times in the past. "See you in a bit."

After he closed the door, Grace grabbed her bag and pulled out running shoes. She glanced at the knife she normally kept hidden in her sock. She didn't need that here. She was safe.

Soon, Grace and Furby were walking along the beach. She unleashed Furby to let him run, and she followed suit.

As she ran, she thought of Brent and the band. She was not going back to New Orleans. Not after what Brent had done. It would put the band in a bind while they looked for a replacement, and she felt bad for her friends, but it was Grace or Brent. And if she went back to New Orleans, one of them would be arrested.

Grace increased her pace to almost grueling. Her heart pounded and her lungs begged for air. She scanned her memory again, hoping to remember what had happened, terrified it was futile. What if she never remembered what happened? What was she going to do?

Finally, she stopped running. She raised her face to the sky and resisted the urge to scream. Taking deep breaths, she waited. She waited until her heart slowed and her breathing became less ragged. She waited for the endorphins to beat out the raging storm in her mind. When it finally calmed, she whistled for Furby and walked back down the beach toward home.

Chapter Three

G race walked through the door to Snapper's and was spotted instantly by Carly.

"Grace!" Carly called as she circled the bar to give her a hug, "Joey didn't tell me you were coming!"

"I surprised him this morning."

"Joey!" Carly called. "Grace is here."

Joey's head poked out of the swinging doors. "Hey, Grace! What can I get you?"

"Get me one of your burgers. Please. And can I get a beer and a shot of Patron? It's been a helluva trip."

"Sure thing," Carly said.

Grace smiled as she spotted Emily, Noah, and Ryder by the bar. After hugs and hellos were exchanged, Grace took a seat next to Ryder.

Ryder was Grace's best friend. He was a long-legged cowboy full of reckless charm. There wasn't a bull he wasn't willing to ride, or a cute woman he wasn't ready to seduce. He lived with Grace off and on in New Orleans when he worked in town.

The chorus of *I'll Be Home for Christmas* filled the bar.

Emily grabbed Ryder. "Wanna dance?"

"Yeah. It's a slow one. You shouldn't be too bad," he said, and she rewarded him with a punch on the arm.

"You wanna dance?" Noah asked Grace after the other two took the floor.

"Nah, you go ahead, I will want to later though."

"Cool."

Noah sipped from his beer for a while. The veteran had never been one to talk much, so they sat and watched the other two dance. About midway through the Christmas carol, he finished his beer. He walked across the makeshift dance floor and tapped Ryder on the shoulder. Ryder smiled and relinquished his dance partner.

Grace took a drink from Carly and drew her knees up to the bar and leaned back. It was her normal pose at the bar. She sat back and absorbed the familiar surroundings. She had grown up in this place. Not the bar; this place hadn't always been a bar. It was a bait shop until Carly and Joey bought it and turned it into Snapper's Bar and Grill. In their younger days, Grace, Benjamin, and Ryder had ridden their bikes here on hot summer days for root beer and their favorite candy. The three of them had been inseparable. Then Ben died. That pain had never gone away. She couldn't imagine what it was like for Noah and Carly to lose a sibling.

Grace sighed and looked around. Neon beer signs covered the walls, advertising mostly American brews. No fancy imports for this crowd. They were a simple, hardworking, honest bunch of mostly males. Colorful posters of past local festivals were framed and placed throughout the bar. A jukebox that played almost constantly because Carly could not stand silence stood against one wall. A single pool table was in front of that. A big screen TV was nestled in the corner and was very popular during LSU and Saints games. That was one time the jukebox did not play. One did not play music during football games. The random newcomer who tried would be quickly chastised and his or her money refunded.

A few regulars littered the main corner of the U-shaped bar. Everyone seemed to have their own spot, and always had. The dominant personalities took the point, and the quieter personalities fanned out from there. It was early, and still happy hour. Later, this group would trickle out and the night crowd would slowly start to filter in.

"Are you okay, Grace?" Carly asked. Carly frequently took the day bartending shift. Grace knew it was because she loved the day crowd, and also it tended to be a bit slower, and she could get some of her clerical and stocking jobs done. As usual, Carly's blonde hair was pulled back, and the pens she used to write orders or keep track of tabs or other business was shoved in the ponytail. By the end of her shift, she would have several tucked in there, and would be looking for one. "You're awfully quiet."

"I'm fine, Carly."

"Are you sure?"

"I'm sure. Thank you."

"Good." Carly raised a blonde eyebrow. That was Carly. She looked out for everyone. That's why everyone loved her.

Ryder left the dance floor and joined Grace at the bar. As usual, he wore a black cowboy hat, boots, and the belt buckle from his latest rodeo win.

He wrapped his arms around her and kissed her forehead. He pulled back and looked her in the eye. When Grace looked up at him, his dark eyes, usually filled with humor, darkened.

"What's wrong?"

"I don't want to talk about it," she said. "Not now."

"Okay. But," he raised an eyebrow, "I'm not letting you off the hook for long. You will tell me what's going on."

"I will. But not today. Not tonight. Drink with me and dance with me," she said. She needed to escape from his prying eyes. She couldn't talk about what happened. Not yet.

He took his cowboy hat off and shoved it on her head. "You got it." He turned toward the bar and propped one cowboy boot onto the rail that surrounded it.

"Some guy do you wrong?" he asked.

Grace flinched, then said, "I thought you were going to leave it alone?"

He turned his barstool to face hers and stared her down. Grace met his glare, unblinking. A stand-off between two strong-willed people; it wasn't the first one, and it wouldn't be the last.

A quick Cajun two-step tune rang through the bar. To distract him, she grabbed Ryder's hand. "Dance with me."

Ryder took her hand and led her through the spirited and complicated traditional dance. Ryder had always been one of the best dancers she had ever partnered with, or even seen dance for that matter. His sure movements on the dance floor had led him to more than one romantic encounter. If it wasn't his smooth moves, it was his charm. He was a shameless flirt. And his dark "Cajun cowboy" good looks didn't hurt either.

When they returned to their stools, Grace's cheeks were red from exertion. Her heartbeat like she'd just performed on stage.

Grace set the cowboy hat on the bar, and Ryder put it back on his head. He lit a cigarette and was quiet. She resumed her normal slouch, drink in hand. Ryder simply let her be, and she appreciated that.

One of the regulars, Evan, came around to their corner of the bar. "Hey, Ryder? Wanna shoot a game?" He gestured to the pool table.

"Sure, man. Rack 'em." Ryder said, getting up to grab a pool stick. He gave Grace's leg a squeeze as he passed.

Grace turned to face the pool game. She watched the two square off on the table and talk smack to each other, and it took her mind off her problems for the time being. Sooner or later, she was going to have to tell Ryder about what happened with Brent. He wouldn't let her get out of that. Not since she had told him every little secret about herself for as long as she could remember. Sometimes, Grace thought Ryder knew her better than she knew herself. He also didn't bullshit. He never minced words or sugarcoated his opinion, and Grace loved that.

Grace smiled as Ryder made a difficult shot. The jukebox died down, so Grace grabbed a five and went to it. She was shuffling through the albums when she felt an arm wrap around her shoulders. She jumped.

She turned to see Joey giving her a funny look. "Grace?"

"Oh, sorry, Joey. You scared me."

"I see that. You okay?"

"Yes, I'm okay," she snapped, and felt bad immediately. "I'm just tired. Too many gigs lately. I need a break."

Joey scanned her face, knowing she wasn't being completely honest, but let it go anyway. He gave her a quick hug. "It's good to have you home, sis."

Joey left her at the jukebox and went to join Ryder in their little corner. Ryder had won the game and was waiting on the next challenger to rack the balls. Grace picked the last few songs and sat back down.

Carly returned with a round of shots. "Here's to our Grace! Carly Bombs and a Patron for Grace!"

Several groaned, "Not Carly Bombs again! I suffered the entire next day!"

"Tough," Carly said. "We don't all get to get together much anymore. Where's Gabe, by the way? Daniel said he was on his way home too."

"He's coming," Joey said. "His band is taking a break until October, so he'll be here a few weeks."

"That's awesome. It's been what? A year since he's been back? His band has really started to take off! And have you seen his pictures? Oh my God! He's so hot!" Carly exclaimed.

"I have." Grace had noticed the difference in his social media pictures as well. He had shaved his goatee and cut off his long, curly brown hair. His new look was more rock, more edgy. More than once, Grace had seen a pic he posted and thought, *Damn, Gabe.*

He wasn't the quiet, soulful artist he had been the last time she saw him.

"What do you think prompted the change?" Grace asked.

"I think it was a woman," Carly said.

"You always think that," Joey said.

"Well, did you ask him?"

Joey's eyes widened. "No. Guys don't ask guys that kind of thing."

Carly rolled her brown eyes. "Ugh. I guess I'll just have to find out the details when he gets here."

"Said he'd see us tomorrow. You can grill him to your heart's content."

"You know I will. And we have another reason to celebrate!"

Carly always looked for a reason to celebrate. Someone was coming home? Celebrate. Saints won? Celebrate. Tuesday? Celebrate. Carly was Grace's polar opposite. Where Grace was dark, Carly was light. One thing they had in common was their love for music, which several of the group shared.

Gabe, Grace, and Benjamin had played together in high school. Benjamin played drums, Gabe the guitar, Grace the bass, and Gabe's friend, Bennett, filled in with guitar and back-up vocals. Their band name back then was Lafitte's Treasure, and they had been convinced they were going to go all the way.

Grace had played with Loup Garou until today. And Benjamin...Grace's heart constricted. What if he had joined one of them in New Orleans, or Austin, instead of taking that job in the oilfield? Would he still be with them?

Grace looked down at her drink that sat on the bar, moisture pooled on the white napkin under the glass. Absently, she turned it in circles, lost in thought.

Ryder nudged her with an elbow. "Whatcha thinking?"

"About Ben," she said.

He exhaled a stream of smoke. "I miss him too."

He clinked his beer bottle with her glass. "Let's go dance. You know Ben would be pissed if we sat around and *carried on* over him."

"You're right. Go play some music."

Grace turned to Emily as he walked away. "How's the catering business going?"

Emily smiled. "It's going so great! I just got some more business from some companies in Lafayette. Word is spreading.

And I've branched out into holiday parties. I'm going to do some Mardi Gras balls too."

Emily was one of those quiet types, not shy, but happy to sit and listen to everyone's conversations. She was perfect for Noah; she was always calm and always steady. Except that one time at the spaghetti cook-off, but that had been her ex-husband's fault. Grace smiled, wishing she would have been here to see Em give that ass the what-for. Carly had messaged her all about it though, and Grace had cheered her from New Orleans.

A fast Cajun tune rang out through the bar. Grace, knowing it was Ryder's music, met him on the dance floor. She took his hand and together they turned circles. She spun until she was almost dizzy. Whether it was from the dance, the drinks, or the lack of good sleep, or a combination of all three, she didn't know.

The song finished, and a slow Cajun waltz came on. She loved waltzes, but Ryder hated them. Too slow for him; he liked the flashier dances. But Ryder would play them every now and then so she could dance. He stepped back, and Noah joined her on the floor.

When he placed his hands on her, she stiffened. Noah's eyes narrowed for a moment.

"You okay?"

Grace shook it off. "Yeah, just jumpy. Too much time in New Orleans, I think."

His dark look told her he wasn't convinced, but he nodded. "Yeah, probably."

He led her through the series of steps and turns, sliding along to the one, two, three step of the music. He was a smooth dancer. Grace had danced with him often in the past and enjoyed it. Stiff at first, by the end of the dance, Grace felt comfortable again.

The song ended and Grace returned to the bar. After two dances, she was parched. She downed the rest of her drink, and Carly quickly replenished it.

The door flashed open and one of Pointe Shade's "boys in blue" walked in. Grace glanced at Carly, who rolled her eyes. Ryder had told Grace that the sheriff, Brent's uncle, Denis Mouton, had taken a liking to Carly and was now making regular appearances. That was a lost cause. Carly and Joey had been fighting their feelings for months now.

Denis Mouton was also known for shady arrests and harassing women. He had been involved in an altercation a few months earlier that ended in a gunshot to his crotch. The official details had never been released.

John, one of the regulars standing at the bar, nodded to the cop. "Hey, Mouton! Dat you?"

The cop took off his dark sunglasses and folded them in his hands. "That's me."

"Good. I tink dat's your game. Dey's one ball left on de table." John nodded to the pool table where one white ball rested on the green table after Ryder and Evan had taken a break from the game.

Grace watched Carly's face twitch in an attempt not to laugh, and when Mouton saw this, his face turned even redder. A vein throbbed in his forehead. His hand went to the baton at his side, as if he wanted to do bodily harm to the offender.

Noah stepped in. "Can we help you, officer?"

Mouton slowly slid his steely grey eyes away from John and over to Noah.

"I'm just making some rounds. I was returning from court in Orleans Parish."

"This isn't your jurisdiction," Noah pointed out.

"True, but I always like to make sure the public is protected, no matter where they're located." Mouton's eyes moved from Noah to Carly. Carly frowned, and turned to a customer and started chatting. Mouton's eyes narrowed at the obvious dismissal. His gaze roamed the room and landed on Grace. He walked over to stand in front of her. Grace felt, rather than saw, Ryder slide to the right just a bit closer to her.

"Well, aren't you the little songbird from New Orleans? Brent's told me all about you. All about you."

Grace's stomach churned at the implication. He knew. She said nothing. She looked down for a minute and fiddled with her black painted fingernails. Her head pounded and her stomach roiled. She refused to let Mouton see her panic.

Finally, she looked back up at his irate glare. He was not used to being dismissed so easily.

"Sir," she said, drawing out the word, "I don't think anyone I know would use the words little or songbird to describe me."

"Oh, and what words would they use?"

Grace's lips twitched, and she looked back down at her fingernails. "Um, I don't know? Sarcastic? Mean?" She looked up and met his eyes again. "A real bitch."

Ryder groaned beside her as Emily spewed her drink across the bar.

"Is that right?" He leaned closer to her face. "Well, in Pointe Shade, we know just what to do with little girls with big attitudes."

Grace leaned in a bit closer. "Try me."

Noah cleared his throat. "As you can see, officer, we are all just perfectly fine here. No drama. I think you can head on back to Pointe Shade now."

Mouton stepped back, his eyes still on Grace. "I think I should. But I'll be seeing you again, soon." He smiled at Grace. "And hopefully in my jurisdiction next time."

Grace shrugged and took a sip of her drink. "Whatever floats your boat."

His hand reached down to his baton again, and in that moment, Grace felt her insides go cold. She refused to look away though and watched as he tipped his hat to Carly and walked out the door.

Grace fought down the bile that threatened to rise by sipping her drink. Not successful, she sat the drink down on the bar. 'I'll be right back."

"Shots are coming," Carly said. "You want to wait a minute?"

"I'll be right back," Grace replied. "Just need a moment."

Carly's eyed her. "What's up?"

Grace forced a smile. "I'm fine, don't worry. I'm just going to the bathroom."

"Okay then," Carly said, although the look she gave Grace said that she knew better.

Grace patted her on the arm and walked away. Once in the bathroom, Grace braced her arms on the vanity. She lowered her head and took a few breaths, hoping to make the sick feeling she had left over from Mouton's visit go away.

"What are you going to do? Who's going to believe you? And don't forget Sheriff Mouton is my dear uncle. I won't pay for anything..." Brent's words echoed in her head. Grace forced down the bile again. Turning on the faucet, she splashed cold water on her face.

"Grace? You okay? You coming? Shots are ready?" Carly's voice was muffled through the bathroom door.

Grace took a deep breath. "Coming."

She turned off the water, took one more cleansing breath, and walked out the door.

Chapter Four

"Grace," Brent's voice echoed beside her ear, his hand cold on her face.

"No," Grace said, shaking her head.

"Grace, you know you want this."

The haze drifted back over her mind, and Brent's face faded away, as well as the feel of his touch.

"No," Grace said as she slept. The sound of her own voice woke her up. She gasped for air and sat up in bed. She was chilled to the bone. She pulled the quilt up and lay back in bed, waiting for her heart to stop racing.

Concerned, Furby licked her nose.

"Ugh, Furb." She patted his furry head and sighed. Slowly, her heart began to slow down. She glanced at the alarm clock by the bed. 5:30 a.m. If she left now, she could take a run down the beach and watch the sunrise.

She kicked off the blankets. "So much for sleeping in."

She donned running shoes and leashed Furby. She left as quietly as she could. She didn't want to wake up Joey and Carly—they'd all been out late celebrating her homecoming.

When she got to the beach, she unleashed Furby and let the energetic dog have his freedom. After a few quick stretches, Grace took off. Grace loved running. She loved the feel of her feet hitting the sand, feeling the power in her legs, the wind in her hair. She felt alive when she ran. In New Orleans, she ran near Jax Brewery and around the Quarter. Running free like this, with no traffic and no people, was heaven.

Grace watched the surf play against the beach, the water coming in, foaming up, then heading back out to sea. The water would be warm now, it being late September. She would probably find herself back on this beach enjoying the cool water along with the tourists and fishermen.

Grace waved to Noah. He was running toward her with his two dogs. Sadie, the German shepherd was his. Oscar, the ugly black-and-white dog with the pointy ears, was Emily's.

Noah slowed as he approached her. "Hi, Grace!" He laughed and held out a hand. "I'd hug ya, but, well..."

"I understand."

"Come over to the house for breakfast if you want when you finish, Emily should be up and cooking."

"Does she ever get tired of cooking?" Grace asked.

"Nope, and I never get tired of eating." Noah laughed, patting his stomach. "That's why I have to run."

Grace looked him over. Noah did not have an inch of fat on his body. He had, however, filled out since a couple of years ago, after he'd gotten back from Iraq. He had lost that almost too skinny look. He looked very happy, and very content.

"Well, I'm not going to keep you. I know you just started your run. But, seriously, stop in and eat. Em would love to see you."

"Got coffee?"

Noah laughed. "Of course we do."

"Let me finish my run and go shower. And I'll stop by if I can."

He placed his hand on her forearm and gave a quick squeeze, and Grace resisted the urge to flinch. What was wrong with her? She'd known Noah for years. *Nerves*, she thought. Something a few days at home should cure.

Noah whistled for his brood of dogs and continued down the beach toward his and Emily's home. Their house had been Emily's grandmother and grandfather's, then she and Noah had restored it after it was damaged by Hurricane Katrina.

Grace continued running. She passed by Aunt Glinda's Redbird Inn, a collection of camps and rooms rented out during the summer season. Aunt Glinda wasn't really Grace's aunt, but that's what everyone called her. Glinda would be busy this morning, making breakfast for the fishermen and families staying there. She would close up after Labor Day. Glinda said retirement wasn't any fun unless you took the time to enjoy it. After Labor Day, she would travel, read, visit, and do just whatever she pleased.

Her grandson, Gabe, had apparently made it in from Austin the night before, as he was standing on the beach, casting a line into the water for some early morning fishing.

"Hey, Gabe!" she said as she approached.

He reeled the line in and turned to her. His full smile was punctuated by a small silver lip ring. He was what you called a beautiful man. His new look had only made him more appealing. His bright, green eyes no longer hid behind a mop of brown curly hair. Now, you could see the sharp angles of his face. The same tattoos he'd had, mostly musical, adorned muscles that popped out from under his t-shirt sleeve.

Damn, Grace thought as he enveloped her in a hug. He, too, had filled out in the last year.

Gabe secured the line on his fishing pole and sat it down.

"Grace!" he said. "How have you been?"

"I've been all right. And you? God, you look great!"

"Thank you," he said. He shrugged. "Our manager said I needed a tougher look, so I went with it."

"Well, it looks great. I bet you have the ladies falling all over you."

He looked down then, his smile disappearing. "I wouldn't say that."

"Well, maybe we can play a few tunes together while you're here. Just like old times."

"Of course," Gabe said. "Grandma should be about finished with breakfast by now, you want to come up? Glinda would love to see you."

"I would, but I just saw Noah, promised him I'd come for breakfast already. In fact, I should head back to shower."

"Okay. Some other time, then."

"Of course. I need to stop in and visit with Glinda anyway."

"Good. Well, I'll see you at Snapper's later?" he asked.

"Yes, you will."

"Grace?" He paused for a moment, and when he spoke again, his voice was deeper than normal. "It's really good to see you again."

Puzzled, she looked into his eyes, the way he was looking at her was different. He looked at her intently, his gaze darker.

Suddenly nervous, Grace looked away from him and down the beach for a moment. When she looked back, the look was gone. Maybe it had been her imagination.

"It was good to see you too," she said, then whistled for Furby, who was running around in the surf. She shook her head. That dog was going to need a good bath after getting dirt and sand in his long, white hair. He ran up to her, paws soaking wet, tongue hanging out the side of his mouth, and did a dance on his two back paws.

Grace laughed and patted his head, "C'mon boy. We're going to have to hurry if I'm going to make it in time for some of Emily's breakfast."

• • • •

GABE WATCHED AS GRACE disappeared down the beach. He'd been crazy about Grace in high school. Had even learned how to play the guitar and ride a motorcycle in an effort to impress her. He remembered mustering up the courage in high school to ask her to the senior prom after practicing in the mirror for days.

"Gabe! Guess what!" Seventeen-year-old Grace's face had glowed with excitement as she ran up to him in the hallway between classes.

"What?" Gabe asked automatically, closing his locker door with a bang and turning toward her.

"The prom committee talked to me this morning. They want us to play for prom!"

"You don't want to go to the prom? It's your senior prom." Gabriel tried to keep the disappointment from showing on his face and in his voice.

"Prom? Me? All that dressing up?" Grace laughed. "You're kidding me. I'd rather play music."

"And what does Ben think? He may have a hot date."

"Ben will line up a date at the prom. You know the girls just love those dimples. He and Ryder might go alone, but they won't leave alone. I promise. Ryder will dance with every girl in the place."

"What are we going to play?" Gabe asked. "I don't think they'll go for a night of Pearl Jam and Nirvana covers."

"I don't know," Grace said. "We need some stuff for people to slow dance to."

"What about some eighties covers?"

"We could do some of those."

Gabe had brightened a little. It may not be a date, but learning new songs meant more practice, which meant more time with Grace. It was a win-win situation for him either way. It also meant she wasn't going with anyone else.

Gabe cast his fishing pole out again and smiled, he had been so awkward as a teen, all gangly and clumsy. He had only been half truthful when he said his makeover was at the request of their new manager. The other half of the truth was Grace. She was the other part of the reason.

The last time he was home, he yearned to do what he'd wanted for years, since he was a teen. He longed to tell her how much she meant to him. Every time he went to make his move, he chickened out, seeing that same old look in her eyes. That "just a friend" gaze had always caused him to freeze up.

Disappointed, he went back to Austin. When he and the band signed their new deal, the manager had made the suggestion to change his look, and he went with it. Maybe a new look in him would inspire a new look from her. This time, he wanted Grace to see him.

He cut his hair, shaved his goatee, hit the gym. If Grace responded half as well as his female fans, he would finally have that chance. When the band went on break, he jumped on his Harley and came home. For Grace. A chance at a new beginning to an old story.

He looked down the beach again toward where Grace had disappeared. Gabriel shy? Not so much now. Quiet? He wasn't going to be quiet this time.

Chapter Five

B ack at the Redbird Inn, later that afternoon, Gabe slid the piano cover open and ran his fingers along the smooth, worn, black-and-white keys. He had learned how to play music on here with Grams looking on and listening. He played a few notes to get the feel for the instrument again. As he played, his mind drifted back to high school when he and Grace would sit here practicing whatever song they were working on at the time.

Automatically, his fingers started playing the old Phil Collins song *Against All Odds*.

He sang softly as his fingers traveled over the keyboard. He had convinced her to sing the song as a duet for the prom, hoping she would see how bad he was crushing on her. But she never had. She had left for New Orleans soon after that to attend the University of New Orleans on a music scholarship. He and Bennett moved to Austin, where there were more opportunities for musicians trying to make it big.

He sang quietly, still playing the old song, hoping Grace would take a look at him now.

"You're still hung up on Grace, aren't you?" Glinda asked from the doorway.

Gabe stopped singing, but not playing, his fingers still as restless as his mind.

"I am."

She smiled and came to sit beside him on the stool. "What are you going to do?"

"I don't know. I saw her on the beach this morning while I was fishing."

"And?"

Gabe thought of the dark circles under Grace's eyes. "I don't know, Grandma. Something seems different."

"Like what?"

"It's a look in her eyes. I don't know. I can't put my finger on it."

"Grace is a tough girl. She'll make it through whatever it is. She does have that soft side though."

He laughed then, "Grace? Soft?"

"She is, Gabe. Look at her with Ryder, or Joey, or that crazy dog of hers. She doesn't love easily, but she loves with all her heart when she does."

He nodded, and suddenly feeling uncomfortable, was quiet.

"Gabriel?" Glinda asked, patting him on the knee. "Since you're here, how about you help me out with some repairs around here? A little hammering and nailing might be what you need to keep that mind of yours occupied. We can give Noah a little break."

He smiled and mentally shook off the past. "Of course, Grams. Just let me know what you need." He slid the piano cover shut and followed Glinda into the kitchen.

• • • •

AFTER BREAKFAST WITH Emily and Noah, and a long nap, it was sunset as Grace walked down the beach, the purple sun mirrored on the water. A light, cool breeze blew, and the feel of the soft sand beneath her toes was comforting.

She walked until she couldn't see anyone else and slid down onto the sand. She sat her drink beside her, after pouring some more vodka into the glass to freshen it up. She pulled her knees up to her chest and turned up her iPod.

Grace looked out at the waves as the sun dipped lower along the horizon. She had resisted going to Snapper's tonight. She did not feel like being sociable. So, she had grabbed her iPod, ear buds, a tall glass of something cold, and wandered down the beach.

She shuffled through to her favorite album, a mournful rock album that was mostly acoustic. The singer sang of sorrow, change, and rock and roll. The album was not cheerful, but Grace was not happy, so it fit her mood.

Feeling her cell phone vibrate, she looked to see who it was.

Ryder: What u doin'?
Grace: Chillin'.
Ryder: Where?
Grace: Beach.
Ryder: Meet me at Snapper's.
Grace: Maybe later.
Ryder: Don't make me come find you.

She set the phone down and sipped her drink. The spot she had picked was perfect. The sun was casting pinks, reds, and oranges across the blue water. It seemed the water itself was on fire.

What was she going to do?

She had sent the band a message earlier telling them she would not be back. She had given them no reason and ignored the ones who had asked. She now had no band, therefore no job, no income. She had some savings built up, but she would still need to pay rent. She couldn't leave her roommate, Paul, in the lurch. She had called him earlier to tell him she would be out for a few days so he wouldn't worry. She would need to tell him soon that he needed to look for another roommate.

She'd talk to Carly later about some gigs. Snapper's booked bands and artists on the weekends. She'd see if Carly could schedule her in. That would do for a little while. Maybe she'd go around to some of the other local places and see if she could get some acoustic gigs. It wouldn't be much. But it would do. She'd been a starving artist before. Of course, here, she'd never really go hungry. You couldn't go anywhere in south Louisiana without someone offering a meal.

She poured more vodka in her glass and took another big drink. She grimaced a little. It was a bit too strong, but as the ice melted it would mellow. With her mood, she was half tempted to just tip the bottle and start drinking. If it had been chilled, she knew she would have.

Grace jumped as a hand touched her shoulder.

She looked up to see Gabe. She was again struck by the changes he had made. She pulled the earbuds out.

"Sorry," he said. "Didn't mean to startle you."

"It's okay. What's up?"

"Nothing. I was just leaving Grandma's to go to my house. You okay?" His bright green eyes were soft.

"Honestly? Nope. I'm not."

"I have some Southern Comfort at my house and some free time. Feel like some company?"

She shrugged. "Knock yourself out."

She saw him bite back a smile. "All right. I'll be right back."

• • • •

GABE WALKED BACK UP to the cabin Glinda kept for him. He had been heading to his place from Glinda's, thinking about going to Snapper's to find Grace, when he had seen her sitting there on the beach. Shoulders slightly bowed, she looked like she was trying to curl up into a ball. He didn't know what was going on with her, but he knew it wasn't good. When he saw her slight intoxication, he knew he couldn't leave her alone. Even if that was what she wanted. He wouldn't push though. He knew her way too well for that. When you pushed Grace, she pushed back. She was a scrapper. Always had been. But with her two best friends being Ryder and Benjamin, she kind of had to be to survive.

He packed an ice chest and headed back to the beach. He approached slowly this time, not wanting to startle her again. He sat the ice chest down between them, giving her space.

"You need a drink?" he asked, then filled her cup when she held it out to him without saying a word.

"Sunset is pretty tonight," he said.

"Yep," she said.

"Talked to Ryder?"

"Yep."

"Want me to call him?" he asked. Maybe Ryder could break her out of this funk.

"Don't you dare." She flashed a look at him, and he mentally threw up his hands.

"Okay," he said. Gabe sipped his drink slowly. This was going to be a long night. He kept talking.

"You know, Carly told me today that they were moving the spaghetti cook-off for Ben's memorial scholarship fund to Labor Day. To be the last hurrah of the season, so to speak. Maybe we can get together and do some songs."

"Maybe so," Grace responded.

She really was in a foul mood. Should he keep talking or just shut up? Knowing Grace, if she wanted him to stop talking, she would say so. So, he kept going. He made small talk about the weather. He talked about fishing. About anything he could think of.

"So, maybe we could all plan a trip to New Orleans, wander down Bourbon?" he asked.

She looked at him then. Her eyes cut to the side, full of rage. She stood up and walked to the surf playing on the shore. Gabriel just watched as she took the cup in her hand and threw it as far as she could out into the water.

"Or maybe not," he said.

She stalked back through the sand and flopped down beside him. She pulled her knees up and wrapped her arms around them.

"You want another drink?" he asked.

She nodded.

"I'll need to get you another cup," he said. "You'll be okay for a minute?"

She nodded again.

Gabriel went back to his cabin and grabbed another cup, a throwaway from last year's Mardi Gras parade. Something he wouldn't miss if she decided to play pitcher again. When he got back, he fixed a drink and handed it to her. He didn't speak again.

Chapter Six

The next morning, Grace woke up with a spinning and pounding head. She groaned, opened one eye, and looked around. She was in Gabe's room.

She grimaced at the taste in her mouth. "What the hell did I drink?" She shook her head, then stopped when it throbbed again. Hangovers were rare for her. Living in New Orleans and keeping weird hours, Grace always liked to keep her wits about her.

She grabbed her cell phone and checked the text messages.

There were three, two from Ryder and one from Joey, who both asked the same thing. "Where are you?" They probably would be frantic, thinking that a random psycho serial killer had gotten her. But what would she tell them?

She was holding the phone in her hands when Gabe poked his head in the room. "How you feeling?"

"Like shit."

He smiled, then replied, "I can imagine."

"I have to text Ryder and Joey."

"I told them where you were. They wanted to come get you, but I told them you'd be all right."

"Oh Lord." She flung a pillow over her head. "I'm so embarrassed."

"You're okay." He crossed over to sit on the foot of the bed. "It happens."

"Not to me. Not that often."

"How about some breakfast?"

Her stomach revolted at the thought. She didn't dare speak. She merely shook her head, still covered by the cool pillow.

"I'll bring back some Sprite and something easy to eat. You'll feel better if you eat a little something."

She groaned.

"I'll be back. Get some rest."

Grace was sleeping before the front door closed.

• • • •

AS GABE WALKED INTO the main area of the Inn, Glinda was putting the finishing touches on the buffet she laid out for breakfast during the season. Biscuits, gravy, sausage, bacon, eggs, and cheese grits were in big silver warmers on a long buffet table that Noah had custom built out of cypress.

Gabe had always loved this room. It had changed a bit over the years as Grams had redecorated every now and then, but the arrangement remained the same. Along one wall was the new buffet, beside that, in the far corner, was a well-stocked bar, also made out of cypress. A fireplace was nestled between two huge bookcases that held books of all genres and board games for families to play. A circle of overstuffed leather chairs sat in front of the fireplace. The rest of the room was filled with small round tables for breakfast, drinks, or small talk. When the weather was nice, Glinda opened the bank of French doors that led out to the deck that faced the water.

An older, speckled gentleman, Daniel, was seated at a table already. Daniel wasn't a customer, he was one of Glinda's friends. They had an unspoken agreement. She fed him during tourist season, and he fed her in the off season. Gabe refused to think about what other unspoken agreements they had, but Gabe knew there were mornings he didn't hear Daniel's car pull in and yet he'd still be at the table, sipping coffee.

Gabe kissed Glinda on the cheek. "Good morning, Grandma."

"Morning, baby. How are you?"

"Good," he said, starting to fill a plate. "Anything in particular you need me to do today?"

"The group in cabin three said the water's not heating up all the way. Can you check on that?"

"Sure thing, Grandma."

"Hi, Daniel," he said, sitting down at the table.

"Hi, Gabe. How are you?" he said and rustled the morning newspaper.

"I'm good."

Glinda, finished with her preparations and fussing, sat down with them for a cup of coffee. It was her ritual almost every morning of the tourist season. When the visitors came in, she would stop to visit with each one. By the time they checked out, Glinda would know where they were from, their names, and almost everything but their social security number. Her ability to make them feel a part of the family was what kept people coming back time and time again.

Daniel took a sip of his coffee. "An officer in Pointe Shade is in trouble."

"That doesn't surprise me. What is it this time?"

Pointe Shade was in St. Andrew Parish, next door to Raphael Parish, in which Bon Chance was located. It was known for ineptitude and corruption. It was like Orleans

Parish's slightly less sophisticated, more redneck younger brother. An example of the good ol' boy system gone bad.

Daniel said, "More inappropriate actions during arrests, traffic stops."

"Something's going to have to give over there. Someone needs to run against Ol' Man Mouton next election." Jacque Mouton was the head of one of the biggest families in St. Andrew Parish, and he ran most of the government offices. He kept his family employed, and with the economy still upset after Hurricane Katrina and an oil spill that had further devastated the coast, he didn't care who he put where as long as his family was taken care of. No matter how unqualified or corrupt.

"True."

Daniel flipped through the paper some more, making small talk with Glinda about local and state politics. Gabe finished his breakfast in silence, thinking of Grace. He wondered again what was wrong with her. What had put those shadows in her eyes? Last night, she had barely spoken three sentences to him. She had sat and drank one drink after another; he hadn't seen her drink like that in a long time. Then there was the Drew Brees throw she had done with her glass. She was angry at something or someone.

Gabe just wished he knew what.

• • • •

AT GABE'S, GRACE ROUSED again from sleep. She exhaled a frustrated breath. She had not been successful at drinking her anger away. It still laid there, coiled like a snake. She could almost taste the poison. Or was it the alcohol? Either way, she had a bad taste in her mouth that didn't seem to be going away.

She lifted her head off the pillow, the rather good smelling pillow, Grace noted as the alcohol fog began to lift. Not an overpowering cologne, a simple scent, like fresh air and ocean water. He wore the same cologne he always had, and she found it familiar and comforting.

Grace heard the door open, Gabe must be back.

Soon, he poked his head in the door with a can of Sprite in one hand and a small, covered bowl in the other.

Since her mouth felt like cotton, she reached for the soft drink. She scooted herself into a sitting position.

"You're too sweet," she said. She sipped on the Sprite. The bubbly sweetness was nirvana. "Ahhhhhh."

"You want to try to eat something?" he asked, holding the bowl up, "I got some biscuits and gravy, some cheese grits, bacon. Glinda has a whole spread at the house if you want to go up there."

"I'll just try the biscuits for now," she said, and he handed her the bowl. He backed away to sit in a chair across from the bed.

"Hey, Gabe?" she said. "Thank you."

"You're welcome, Grace." He looked down and chewed his bottom lip for a second. "I know you have Ryder and Joey, but I'm here too if you need someone to talk to."

Grace's stomach twisted, and it wasn't because of the biscuit or the Sprite. She couldn't talk to any of them. Ryder would get angry and want to fight Brent, and probably even-tempered Joey would also. That would only add to her humiliation. This was something she was just going to have to sort out on her own. What could they really do anyway? What was done, was done.

She glanced up at him and smiled. "Thank you. Again."

"Anything for you."

She tore the biscuit apart and munched on it. "I'll finish this up and get out of your hair."

"No rush. I need to shower and get ready to help Glinda. But stay as long as you need."

"I need to get back. My dog is probably wondering where I am."

"'Kay. If you'll wait until I'm ready, I'll drive you back."

"Nah. I'll just walk. It will be good for me. Maybe I can sweat out some of this alcohol."

"'Kay." He went into the bathroom and closed the door. Grace heard the shower start.

Grace took a last bite of biscuit and a few more sips of the Sprite. She needed to get home. She took a moment to tidy up.. Then, took off toward Joey's.

It was already warm as she walked down the beach. The sun beat down on her face, making her sweaty and even more nauseous. Midway to Joey's, she gave up and sat on the cool sand for a moment.

She really should have taken Gabe up on his offer. At least his truck would have been air-conditioned. She took a deep breath. Last night was not a good idea. Instead of feeling better, she felt worse. She'd head home, sleep this hangover off, then go talk to Carly about some gigs. She'd make something out of this crappy day. What did all those self-help people say? Think positive and good things will come to you?

Whatever. The thought made her head pound.

She listened to the waves as they softly hit the sand, the soothing sounds punctuated by the calling of the sea gulls. She closed her eyes and took a deep breath of the cool, salty air. It felt good to be home.

She sat there, simply enjoying the smells, the sounds, the warmth of the sun. Until the sun became too warm again, then she pushed herself back up and continued to Joey's.

When she walked in, Joey was sleeping on the couch. He had been waiting for her. Great, she thought. She tried tiptoeing. It didn't work. He sat up as soon as she stepped in the room.

"Grace? You okay?" he asked.

"Joey. I'm fine. You didn't have to wait for me. I was with Gabe."

"That's what he said. Ryder and I said we'd come get you."

"I know. I was okay."

"I'm worried about you," he said.

"I'm just hungover. I need sleep. Then some good and greasy food. You cooking at Snapper's today?"

"Yeah."

"Go back to sleep. I need to walk Furby, then I'll go to bed and come up to Snapper's later for lunch. A Joey Special already sounds incredible. And I need to talk to Carly about some gigs."

"So, you're sticking around for a little while?" he asked.

"It seems that way."

"What about the band?" he asked.

"What about it?" she snapped.

"Okay..." he said. "Carly would love to book you, I'm sure. Everyone always enjoys hearing you play."

"I'm sorry, Joey. Just cranky today. Too much vodka last night, and whatever it was Gabe was drinking."

"I understand." He smiled. "I'll see you a little later. I walked Furby earlier, by the way. He should be fine."

"Oh, thank goodness. I really just want to lay back down."

"You're welcome," he said, smiling. "Now, Grace the Grouch, go back to bed so we can stand you later."

"Oh, that's my plan," she said, and walked down the hall to her room.

• • • •

GRACE WOKE UP LATER that afternoon, feeling better, but only in a slightly better mood. At least her head wasn't pounding anymore. After showering, her belly growled. The biscuit she had eaten earlier had worn off. She hadn't eaten anything for dinner last night, hence the extreme intoxication and hangover. She knew better than that.

Soon, she was walking into Snapper's. Even at noon there were already a few patrons around the bar. Snapper's was often a gathering place for the retired fishermen and oilfield workers in town. Daniel was there. He would go by Glinda's, have breakfast, read the paper, then head to Snapper's to visit. It was his daily routine. There were a couple of other customers in there as well. People Grace didn't know. She hugged Daniel and sat beside him.

"What's up, pretty lady?" he asked her.

"Not much. Starving," she said.

"What do you want for lunch?" Carly asked, putting a Coke in front of her. Carly already knew what she wanted to drink. That was what made Carly a great bartender. She knew her customers well.

"I want a Joey Special," she said. The Joey Special was a thick hamburger with pepper jack cheese, extra pickles, and a spicy Cajun mayonnaise. It was the perfect cure for a hangover. "And extra fries."

"You got it," Carly said, disappearing through the swinging doors to the kitchen.

"So, what have you been up to, Grace?" Daniel asked her.

"Not much. Still playing music in New Orleans, or was. Had that regular gig going on. But that didn't work out." Grace found herself saying more than she intended to, but Daniel had that effect on people. Grace often thought he was something like the "Problem Whisperer." You spend five minutes with him, and Daniel would know all your problems. You had to be careful around him, or you'd end up feeling like you'd just seen a shrink.

"Oh?" he asked.

Grace smiled. She wasn't falling for it. "Yeah. You had breakfast with Glinda this morning?"

"Of course."

"How's she doing?" Grace asked.

"She's good. You should go see her soon."

"I will."

"What's up today?" Carly asked, returning from the kitchen.

"Not much."

"So, you hung out with Gabe last night?" Carly said, grinning. "Wanna tell me about it?"

Grace shook her head. "Oh, no, you don't."

Carly blinked and tried to look innocent. "Don't what?"

"No matchmaking. Absolutely not."

"But it worked out so well for Emily and Noah!"

"You didn't do crap for Em and Noah," Grace said, laughing, "They already had a past and were perfect for each other."

"See?"

"No."

"We'll see," Carly said, grinning again.

Grace almost sighed in relief when a bell dinged in the kitchen, signaling that food was in the window. Soon, Carly was returning with a plate full of Joey goodness. The smell was incredible. And just what Grace needed to settle her stomach. Carly grabbed a handful of fries from Grace's plate and munched on them.

Henry, an oilfield worker on his two weeks off, came up then. He shook Daniel's hand, said hi to Grace, and gave Carly an over-the-counter hug.

"Did you read the paper this morning?" he asked Daniel.

"I did."

"Did you read about that officer over in Point Shade? About him touching on those women?"

"I did."

"What the hell?" Henry asked. "Isn't that the same one who shot himself in the balls last year?"

"Yes, it was Denis Mouton," Daniel said. "He's old man Mouton's grandson. Probably needed a job, so they outfitted him with a badge and a gun. Probably shoulda just given him a taser. 'Course he may've tased himself."

"Denis?" Henry asked. "The cop who comes around here every once in a while?"

Carly grimaced as she walked up, overhearing the conversation. "Oh God. That guy? Ugh. He thinks he's God's gift to women. Arrogant little prick. And he's married! That poor woman. Having to put up with that."

How she had missed these people!

"Carly, you have any nights open that I could play?"

Carly frowned. "Not this month. I always book at least a month in advance. But I can grab the calendar and see what we might have next month?"

"That would be great."

Carly disappeared into the storage room/office at the back of the bar and returned with a large calendar. She flipped to the next month and handed it to Grace. "Just write your name in on the open dates you want, and we'll go from there. Will Gabriel be sitting in too?"

"If he wants to."

"Oh, I think he will," Carly said with a smile.

Grace frowned again, then turned her attention to the calendar. Carly pulled one of the numerous pens from her blonde ponytail and handed it to Grace, "The Wahoo and 31 also book music. If you want to wait until my shift is over, I'll take a ride with you and we can see if we can get some other days for ya."

Grace thought of the run-in with Mouton and frowned again. "I'll skip 31 for now." It just so happened 31 was in Mouton's jurisdiction. Grace didn't back down from a fight, but she didn't go looking for trouble either.

Carly frowned. "Maybe you're right. I don't relish a run-in with any Moutons. But definitely the Wild Wahoo. I'll give the others a call and we can make a night out of it."

"Sounds good."

"Ryder staying in your place in New Orleans?" Carly asked. When Ryder worked in New Orleans, he often slept on Grace's couch to keep from having to drive back and forth every day.

"Nah, he said he didn't want to stay if I wasn't there. He said it didn't feel right."

"Then he can come too!" Carly said. "Yea! We haven't all been together in forever."

Carly glanced at the clock. "Still a couple of hours of my shift left. You think you can just hang out?"

"Sure."

"Awesome! When I get finished, I'll run home and take a quick shower and we can hit the road. We'll get Noah to be our DD, and we'll be good. I just bought this killer pair of heels I've been dying to try out."

"You? Heels?" Grace raised an eyebrow. Carly wore flip-flops ninety percent of the time. Five percent of the time she was barefoot. The rest was Carly trying to wear heels. It never worked.

"What? We're going out. I may see a hot guy," Carly said.

"In Bon Chance?" Grace raised an eyebrow.

"You never know."

"This should be interesting. You showing cleavage too?" Grace said, eyeing her over her Coke.

"You bet. You ready for a real drink?"

"Sure, why not?"

Carly brought her a Sprite and vodka, then left to take care of the rest of the patrons. Grace turned her attention to Daniel.

"What are we going to do with her?" Grace asked him.

"I have no clue," Daniel said with a laugh.

"So, Grace," Daniel began, "what are your plans?"

"Plans?"

"You staying here? Going back to New Orleans?"

"Not going back to New Orleans."

"So, your options are open, then?"

"Completely."

"I'll keep an eye out for jobs I think you might like. Ever thought about doing anything with that college degree you have?"

"Honestly, I haven't given much thought to anything yet. It's only been a couple of days."

"I'll look. Surely we can find something."

Grace smiled. "I'm sure we can."

Daniel turned the conversation to small talk, and they conversed lightly until Carly's shift ended. Carly turned the bar over to Amanda, the evening bartender, and soon was headed home to shower, change, and drag Joey out. They would all meet here, except for Ryder, who was driving in from New Orleans, then head out.

Emily and Noah showed up together, followed by Gabriel. As he walked in, Grace was struck again by what a good-looking man he had turned out to be. He had a new confidence that was intriguing.

Hellos and hugs were exchanged, drinks ordered. Emily sat next to Grace, and Grace was grateful for the female's company. She never asked too many questions, didn't pry, didn't try to fix you up with someone. No stress with Em, and Grace liked it.

Gabe took the other seat next to Grace. "How you feeling?"

Grace laughed. "Much better."

"You looked pretty rough this morning."

She punched him in the arm. "Thanks. I felt it too."

"You're welcome."

"Thanks also for bringing me the food and the Sprite. I think it saved my life. That walk home was rough though."

"I told you I would have taken you home."

"I know. I'm stubborn sometimes."

"Sometimes?" He raised one eyebrow.

She punched him in the arm again. "Hush ya mouth. On another note, I scheduled some gigs with Carly for next month. You want to sit in with me? Like old times?"

He smiled again. "Of course."

"Good."

Carly arrived with Joey in tow. He was already frowning. Grace shook her head. Some things never changed.

Carly teetered, rather than walked, over to the group.

"Heels, Carly?" Noah asked.

"Yes. And don't roll those faceballs at me."

"Faceballs?"

"I read it on Facebook. It's another way to say eyes. And the heels? A girl needs to wear heels every now and then," Carly said.

"Fine," he said. Grace thought again how nice it was to see him smile so much. When she had come in for Ben's memorial and to get Snapper's going, he didn't smile much at all. Life had been good to him, and Grace felt a slight twinge in her stomach. Jealousy or hope? She didn't know.

"Everyone ready?" Carly asked. "We may need another driver. Anyone game?"

Gabe volunteered. "I'm in Gram's truck, so I can only fit two or three."

"That's fine. Grace, why don't you ride with Gabe? I think the rest of us can fit in Emily's SUV."

Grace shot Carly a look. Grace couldn't get out of it now without making the situation awkward. She did not need Carly matchmaking for her. Not now.

Arrangements made, they all headed out to the cars. Carly was last, wobbling on her high heels.

"Wait!" Carly called, her heels beating an uneven rhythm across the bar's wooden floor and outside. Grace watched as she grabbed onto the porch's railing to keep from plummeting down onto the ground.

Grace looked over to see Joey's grim face. There would be an argument tonight between the two. She could already tell.

The ride to the Wild Wahoo wasn't a long one, and soon they were pulling into the parking lot. Grace was always amused by the big pink fish sign on the roof.

They all bounded into the bar at the same time. Carly and Emily went to get drinks as the rest of them secured a table near the jukebox and pool tables.

"Damnit," Joey said, pulling up a barstool and surveying the crowd. "Cecily is here."

A collective groan came from the men. Grace smiled. If you looked up the word cougar in the dictionary, there would be a picture of Cecily seductively stretched out in leopard print spandex.

Joey elbowed Grace. "Don't make eye contact. She'll take that as an invite. Last time we ran into her, I left here violated."

"Violated?" Grace asked, raising an eyebrow.

Ryder laughed. "She grabbed him under the table. And licked his arm."

"You laugh. I'm siccing her on you this time," Joey said.

"I'm not scared of her," Ryder said. "Besides, she has a thing for you, not me."

"You will be before she's done with you."

Emily and Carly returned with the drinks and took seats. The guys put up quarters on the pool table and grabbed cue sticks.

"Dollar for the jukebox?" Carly asked, and everyone dug into their pockets for music money.

"No cheesy crap," Joey said.

Grace shook her head, she didn't know why Joey even said it. Carly was sure to play some godawful '80s or '90s tune just to aggravate him now. Would it be *Macarena*? *Baby Got Back*? Or something worse?

"Play something slow," Noah said as he gave her his money. "I'd like to dance with my beautiful woman tonight." Noah wrapped an arm around Emily and hugged her close. Emily responded by smiling and resting her head on his shoulder for just a moment.

"I don't know why y'all tell me what you want to hear, I already know," Carly said smiling. "Y'all should just trust me."

Carly turned her attention to the jukebox, and the guys started their pool game. Grace went to talk to the bartender to find out about setting up some gigs. Soon, the manager came out, and Grace walked back to the table with a smile, having set up two gigs at the Wahoo. With the two she'd scheduled at Snapper's, she now had something planned for every weekend. Things were definitely looking up.

The last few notes of the slow rock song Carly had played wound down, and Carly giggled. *Here we go*, Grace thought. Carly always giggled when she played a truly horrendous song.

"*Ice, Ice Baby*?" Joey asked. "I'm not giving you any more money."

Carly laughed. "I've got my own money. And I have a whole list of horrible eighties songs, just to torment you."

Grace resisted the urge to stab herself in the ear. She sipped her drink while watching the crowd and her friends. It felt good to be home and to be away from the craziness of the Quarter. To not have to be on guard all the time. She loved New Orleans and the Quarter, but it was good to relax too. Maybe this was what she needed. Maybe she had just been too wound up for too long. Maybe this had nothing to do with Brent.

A slow Cajun song started to play, and Noah reached out for Emily. She smiled and took his hand and let him lead her to the dance floor.

Gabe, who had been with the guys playing pool, walked up to Grace. "Dance?"

"Sure," Grace said, never one to turn down a trip around a dance floor.

Grace took his hand, his other rested on her hip, and they rocked to the slow beat of the music. Grace's hand settled on his arm, and she was surprised again by the muscle she felt underneath the soft fabric of his t-shirt.

They didn't talk as they circled the dance floor, soon to be joined by Carly and Joey. Awkward was the best word to describe the stiff shuffling those two were doing. As if neither wanted to get too close. Carly's heels didn't help.

Gabe nudged her then and tilted his head to see Ryder dancing with Cecily. Or rather, Ryder trying to dance as Cecily groped him. In the dim light, you could clearly see her bright red nails splayed across Ryder's dark jean clad backside.

Cecily leaned in close to Ryder's ear and whispered something, and Ryder looked at Joey and laughed. Grace could only imagine what she had said. That woman was actually more shameless than Ryder.

The song ended, and Grace grimaced again as another cheesy '80s song played. Ryder and Noah returned to the pool tables. Gabe, instead of joining the rest of the guys, took a seat next to Grace.

"No more pool?" Grace asked.

"Nah, not really my thing," he said.

"Me either. I've tried to play a couple of times, and I just don't have the patience for it. Have you ever watched Carly play?" Grace asked.

"Yes." He smiled. "That girl can't even hit the white ball."

"She gives it a good try though."

"Yes, she does."

Grace looked out at the guys playing pool, absently playing with the charm bracelet she'd had since high school.

"You still have that bracelet?" Gabe asked.

Grace smiled. "Yeah."

"Can I see?" he asked.

"Yeah," she said, holding her arm out so he could get a better look.

He held her hand gently in his as he flipped through the charms. "Angel wings?" he asked, raising an eyebrow.

She laughed. "Zombie hunter."

He laughed. "Now, that makes sense."

"You haven't seen *The Walking Dead*?"

"Nah, I'm not big on zombies. Give me a good action show or some sci-fi."

"You have to see it. It's so good. The characters alone are awesome."

"The zombies? I can't see how."

Grace broke the contact to point to the pool table where Joey and Ryder were trying to play a game of pool. It appeared Cecily had other plans. She was busy trying to drape herself over Joey, and he was busy trying to extricate himself from her grasp.

Carly intervened then. "Let me go save Joey."

"We gotta watch this!" Grace said to Gabe as Carly walked away.

Carly wobbled slowly to the pool table.

"Shit!" she exclaimed as her ankle turned and she fell forward toward the pool table.

Joey lunged to catch her but was too late. The smack as she hit the ledge of the pool table could be heard throughout the bar.

"Damnit, Carly!" Joey said as he reached out to her. Carly turned to him, cradling her arm to her chest.

"Let me see," he said. Carly held out her arm where there was already an angry red bruise.

"I told you to not wear those shoes," Joey scolded her as he turned her arm gently to look at it.

She yanked her arm back and grimaced. "Shut up, Joey."

Joey looked up at the rest of them. "Are you guys ready to go? We should probably get her back and get some ice on that. I have a pack of peas in the freezer I keep just for her."

They nodded and filed out the door.

Chapter Seven

Grace walked up the wide front porch of the Redbird Inn. She stomped soggy feet on the welcome mat and hung her soaked hoodie on the rack by the door. The weather was terrible, rainy and stormy, but she had promised Gabe and Glinda that she would make it for breakfast. She didn't knock on the door. No one did in the morning. It was well known that Glinda's door was open for breakfast every morning during the season.

"Grace!" Glinda exclaimed when she saw her come through the dining room door. She went to Grace and hugged her tight.

"How are you, girl? We've missed you. Haven't we missed her?" she said, nodding at Gabe and Daniel, who were already sitting at the table.

"C'mon, girl. Have a seat," she said before they could answer, and pushed Grace toward the empty seat near Gabe. "Let's look at you."

She looked Grace up and down. "Pretty as a picture, as always," she said. "But you need some meat on those bones. You are way too skinny. Haven't you been eatin' in Nawlins? I know they have good places to eat. Why, I was just telling Daniel the other day that we needed to go up there soon and go eat at one of those restaurants. I've been closed up in this place long enough. I need some Bourbon Street and Garden District in my life."

Grace looked at Gabe and smiled. When Glinda got started, you just kind of went with the flow. Eventually, she would wind down and you could chit chat.

"What do you want to eat? I'll fix it for you."

Grace started to say, "Surprise me," but knew she'd better not. Glinda would put a lot of everything on her plate, and Grace did not feel like leaving this morning feeling like Godzilla after a New York City buffet.

"I'll fix it," Grace said, getting up. "You sit down and have some coffee."

"Okay, dear. If you're sure."

"I am. Thank you though."

Grace fixed a plate and had a seat beside Gabe.

"Mornin'," he said.

"Mornin'." She nodded to Daniel.

Grace began to dig into the plate she had made. Cheese grits had always been a favorite of hers, and she had piled on a good portion of those. Bacon, scrambled eggs, and a biscuit with a side of Glinda's homemade strawberry jelly rounded out the plate.

"Mornin', pretty lady," he replied, rustling the newspaper. "Seems like a teacher in Pointe Shade was found wandering in the city park last night."

"Really?" Glinda asked. "Well, that's bizarre."

Daniel began to read aloud from the paper. "Last night in St. Andrew Parish, Pointe Shade officers found Andre Thibodeaux in Huey Long Municipal Park at approximately ten o'clock. According to reports, Mr. Thibodeaux was found wearing only ladies' underclothes and red lipstick."

"Well, that's interesting," Gabe said. "Aren't you looking for a job, Grace? You did get a degree in education."

"I am not teaching," Grace said.

"It would be steady work," Glinda said.

"I am not teaching. I don't want to teach. That internship experience in New Orleans was bad enough."

"Okay," Gabe said, "but I think you would be good at it."

"What would I teach?" Grace said. "Look at me and do the exact opposite? No."

"Well, just keep it in mind. They'll need someone pretty quick. I doubt Mr. Thibideaux will be coming back," Daniel said.

Grace sipped her coffee. "I'll think about it," she said. *When hell freezes over*, she thought. She had the gigs coming up. She could do those and hopefully schedule some more. She would get by somehow. Without stepping into a classroom.

"You going to Snapper's tomorrow night? We can do some karaoke," Gabe said.

Grace was grateful for the change of subject. "Probably," she said, "but we're not doing any cheesy *I Got You Babe* songs. I'm no Cher, no."

"I can deal with that." If Ryder was the dancer, Gabriel was the singer. He had a voice as smooth as cane syrup. They often sang karaoke when she was in, or if she was playing, Gabe would often sit in for a few songs. A favorite of theirs was *Broken* by Amy Lee and Seether. A song she still performed.

They had never been ones to do *Summer Lovin'*, *I've Had the Time of My Life*, or any other song they would consider to be a cheesy duet. They left that to the tourists.

Grace finished her coffee and went to the kitchen to put her dishes in the sink. "I'd better get going. I need to call some places Carly told me about for some gigs. Thank you so much for breakfast, Aunt Glinda."

"You're very welcome, girl. Come back anytime," she said.

She hugged Glinda, then Daniel and Gabe before she left.

She hoped she could find some more jobs soon. Her funds were not going to last forever.

• • • •

GABE LAY ON THE COUCH in his cabin, flipping through the selections on the streaming video channel. He passed all the versions of *Star Trek*, serial killer shows, motorcycle gang shows, but nothing caught his attention. He'd either seen them all or just wasn't in the mood. *Must be the weather*, he thought. He wasn't one to watch a lot of TV. He preferred to be outside or busy, but the torrential rain kept him from doing much of anything.

The zombie show Grace loved so much caught his attention. He read the summary again. He thought again of cradling Grace's slender wrist in his hand, of that charm bracelet. *Why not?* He clicked on the first episode. Within minutes, he was hooked. Without taking his eyes off the TV, he grabbed the phone to text Grace.

Gabe: Watching ur zombie show.
Grace: Oh really?
Gabe: Yep.
Grace: Whatcha think?
Gabe: It's good. What u doin?
Grace: Not a damn thing.

Gabe: Wanna come watch?
Grace: I could.
Gabe: Awesome. Will pause it.
Grace: Just know. This is no Netflix and chill.
Gabe laughed and replied, *Of course not.*
Grace: LOL. C ya soon.

Gabe paused the show and shot up off the couch. He needed to put on pants and straighten up before Grace arrived. Not that it was messy, but he needed to toss dirty clothes in the washing machine. He should do a few other minor masculine touch ups, like put the toilet seat down and rinse the sink. He had just finished everything when Grace knocked.

He opened the door, and his heart beat a little faster. Her dark hair was in a sloppy ponytail, wet tendrils escaping the elastic and framing her slim, pale face. She wore simple yoga pants and what looked to be one of Joey's old Saints t-shirts. Her demeanor was still tough and rugged, though, and the dark smudges under her smoky eyes testified to a lack of sleep. He found the temptation to touch her, if only for comfort, almost impossible to resist.

"Come on in out of the rain," he said, holding the door open wide.

"'Kay."

She ducked through the door, took her shoes off, and padded across the living room area. She settled into the brown, overstuffed armchair, the only place to sit in the living room other than the couch. She pulled her feet underneath her and put a pillow in her lap, holding it like a shield.

The TV was still paused where he had left it. One of the main characters was on the screen, fending off the attack of a half-decomposed zombie.

"You're still early in the show!" she exclaimed.

"Yes, and you are right. It's definitely catchy."

"You haven't even met Shaggy," she said.

"Shaggy?"

"The squirrel hunting redneck. He's my favorite," she said, and held up her wrist to point to the dangling angel wings. "Shaggy wears a leather vest with angel wings. You'll see."

He nodded slowly. "Ahhh, okay."

Gabe crossed over to the couch and sat down. He hit play, and the show resumed. The man fended off the zombie attack with some help from the ragtag group of survivors, and the show went on to the next catastrophe.

Gabe looked over at Grace on occasion and was amused to see her hold up the pillow near her face when certain characters were in danger. She still reacted, even though she knew what was going to happen.

When the next episode ended, he stood up and stretched. "Do you want something to drink?" he asked, needing something himself.

"What are you drinking?" she asked.

"Southern and Seven."

"I'll take the same," she said.

"Awesome."

He went to the kitchen and made two drinks. He set hers on the small table next to the chair.

"Thank you."

"You're welcome. So, how far into the series are you?" he asked.

"Far. You won't believe what happens. I will warn you, don't get too attached to any characters. There's a good possibility they won't make it."

"Is that right?"

"Yep, you'll see. But enough talking, put the show back on," she said.

"Well, all right then," Gabe said with a laugh, and clicked on the next episode.

Hours later, after many more zombie attacks, and more than a few characters lost, Gabe looked over at Grace. She was sleeping, still clutching the pillow to her chest. In the dim light from the lamp, he could see tears trickling down her cheeks. His heart constricted in his chest and he got up to kneel next to her. Gently, he stroked her hair. He bit his bottom lip to keep the words he wanted to say at bay, afraid he would wake her. Terrified he'd say too much.

When she seemed to be calm again, he grabbed one of Glinda's blankets from the end of the sofa and covered her. He reached out and caressed her cheek, then he turned the lamp off beside the chair and clicked on another episode.

• • • •

GRACE WOKE WITH A START, eyes wide, heart beating furiously. She looked around in the dim haze of the light from the TV. Gabe was sleeping on the couch. Resting, he looked less tough rocker and more like the guy she remembered. Sitting up, she stretched out kinks that had resulted from napping upright.

Hearing her stir, Gabe roused too. He sat up on the sofa, stretched, and grabbed his phone off the guitar-shaped coffee table.

"What time is it?" Grace asked.

"Nine o'clock."

Grace stood up and stretched again, still feeling the effects of sleeping on the chair. She walked through the cabin to the restroom. When she returned, Gabe was in the kitchen.

"Hungry?" he asked.

"A little."

He nodded. "I'll see what I got. Why don't you put on some music?"

"Sounds good. Music, I can do. Cooking, not so much," Grace said, and Gabe smiled.

"I don't cook much either, but I'm sure I can whip up something."

Grace crossed over to the stereo system. It was a state-of-the-art system with the works, an iPod docking station, and surround sound speakers. An extensive vinyl record collection was housed in shelves underneath the system. *A lost art*, Grace thought, pulling some of the covers out and running her hands over them. Old Foreigner, ZZ Top, and even *Urban Cowboy*. Seeing that album, she smiled.

Gabe's tastes were as wide as her own. Like Grace, Gabe also picked up albums for pure entertainment. Although Grace doubted that he owned the Village People like she did. Grace had never actually listened to the album, but it was fun to have in her collection.

Grace settled on an old Van Morrison album and powered the record player on. She set the needle on the record, loving the sound of the familiar scratch as the needle hit the vinyl. The gentle, soothing sounds of the old music rang through the small cabin. Grace returned to the kitchen area and took a seat on a barstool. As she did, Gabe set a glass in front of her.

"Good choice," he said, indicating the music.

"Thank you. It's mellow."

"And perfect after a stormy, zombie evening." He smiled again. The silver lip ring flashed in the light, and Grace's stomach fluttered just a little. His green eyes met hers, and, nervously, Grace looked down at her drink.

"I've always loved *Into the Mystic*," Grace said, 'but it's a song I've never performed on stage or karaoke."

"I don't think I have either," Gabe said. "It's like one of those old classics you hear and think, 'Man, what a great song!' and then it's gone again."

"You're right."

"Maybe we'll have to change that at Snapper's one night."

"Maybe so," Grace said. Glancing down again, she saw the *Urban Cowboy* album she had carried over with the rest of the albums. She picked it up and showed it to Gabe.

"Look! It's Ryder! Same black cowboy hat, black hair, everything. I never realized he looks like a young John Travolta. That chest hair though!"

Gabe laughed and reached out for the cover. "You know, you're right!"

"Lookin' for love in all the wrong places," Gabe said. "That could be Ryder's theme song."

"Yes, it definitely could," Grace said, smiling. Although they both knew that what Ryder was looking for wasn't love.

"I tell you what," Gabe said, handing her a pen and pad of paper, "why don't you start a list of songs, and we can start a set list."

"Awesome. I can do that. We can branch away from the eighties hair bands and bar songs I've been doing with the other band. Try something new, for me, anyway."

"You do that, and I'll start cooking. Feel free to look over the records. Or," he said, sliding his phone over to her, "you can see what I have on my phone."

"The first two have to be *Into the Mystic* and *Looking for Love*," Grace said, writing the titles down on the pad. "Let me go see what else you have. To make it more fun, we have to listen to them too."

She slid off the barstool and went back to the corner that housed the record collection. She pulled out a bright blue album. "Journey, of course," she said, laying that album aside. *Faithfully* was a favorite of hers, and Gabe's raspy rocker voice would give it an edgy makeover. Grace would text Carly later and ask if she wanted to schedule in an '80s night. Carly would love the big hair and neon. Grace remembered that Carly had hosted theme nights before with success. Nothing like reliving high school memories, Grace supposed, grateful her teens had been a bit more edgy. Grace thought of her teasing her own hair and cringed. She was more Joan Jett than Debbie Gibson.

"Oooh!" Grace said, scribbling down some Joan on the list. She was sure Gabe didn't have the album, but Grace had it on her iPod. Grace continued going through the albums, grabbing a few and adding more to the pile, and putting some back. Some wouldn't do.

When finished, she carried the treasures back to the bar and laid them down before taking a sip of her drink. Gabe had resumed his work in the kitchen and was busy with pots and pans.

"Whatcha cookin?" Grace asked.

"I thought some good old comfort food, after the rain and all. A little shrimp and sausage jambalaya and some potato salad. Simple enough."

Grace took another sip of her drink. "Simple for you maybe. I'm just one step above Carly in the kitchen skills department. Boxed spaghetti or macaroni and cheese is about the best I can do."

Gabe laughed. "You think I had a chance of growing up with Glinda and *not* being able to cook at least a little. She still sends me care packages to Austin! Like I'm starving or something."

Grace smiled. "She loves you."

"Yes, she does, and I love her," he said, continuing to cut onions, bell peppers, and celery, the trinity of Cajun cooking. Every recipe known to Cajun man started with those three ingredients.

He nodded to the pile of records. "You found some good stuff?"

"I did."

"Great. You keep the music going, and we can add or cross off. After we eat, I'll grab my guitar and we can see what we got."

Grace nodded. "Sounds like a plan."

Grace watched as he looked at her, chewing on his bottom lip. She could see the questions flicker across his face. Grace stiffened. She looked away, to stare at the front door. She could leave now. Make some excuse. She was tired. It was late. It was easier than staying and awkwardly avoiding questions. She got enough of those from Joey and Ryder.

Gabe reached out and gestured to the albums in front of her. "Tell me you have some women in mind as well. It can't just be all men. You need some time to shine."

Grace exhaled a breath, relieved. "Of course I do."

She pulled out a Fleetwood Mac album. "Not sure of any of these, but we can take a listen. I'm thinking more Stevie Nicks."

"Of course." He went back to chopping vegetables, and Grace resumed her comfortable slump on the stool. She continued flipping through the records, making notes, stopping to hum a few bars of songs to get the feel for the lyrics, the rhythm.

Gabe continued cooking, stopping occasionally to make a comment on a song, an artist, or make a recommendation to keep a song or cut it. Before Grace knew it, she was more relaxed than she had been in days. Maybe she had just needed some music therapy.

Grace leaned back on the stool and exhaled a deep breath. "Looks like we have quite a list going. We have some work cut out for us. We'll have to run through them a few times."

"That's fine," Gabe said. "I got nothing but time." He looked up from the cutting board and Grace was struck by the look she saw in his eyes. A glint she had never noticed before from him. Attraction.

Shocked, she looked down at her drink again. It was empty. "I need a refill."

"I'll get it," Gabe said when she started to get up.

"It's okay," Grace said.

"I haven't seen you this relaxed since you got here, Grace," he said, his green eyes narrowing and piercing into hers. "Let me do it. You take it easy."

Grace smiled. She pushed the glass forward. "You win."

"This one," he said.

He refilled the glass and set it in front of her. He pulled up the lid on the heavy cast iron pot that sat on the gas stove. The spicy scent of Cajun cooking wafted through the kitchen.

"Almost done," Gabe said, setting the lid back down after a quick stir to keep the rice from sticking. Satisfied all was well, Gabe set some plates and utensils out on the bar, refilled his drink, and finished readying the meal.

He hummed along with the music, filling the plates as the food finished. They spent the meal talking about music. They compared notes about bands they had seen live, which ones were on their bucket lists to see, and about music festivals they hadn't been to yet, but wanted to go to. Like the Festival Acadien in Lafayette that featured local bands, artists, and cuisine.

As the meal and conversation progressed, Grace felt herself relax even more.

"That was awesome," she said, pushing the plate forward. "I'm stuffed."

She took another sip of her drink and leaned back on the barstool. "Still want to try out some of those songs?"

Gabe grinned. "Yes, I would. You wanna go outside? Maybe light a fire?"

"That sounds great. You want me to help you pick up?"

"Nah, I'll get it."

"You sure?"

"Positive."

"'Kay," Grace said, carrying a drink outside. She had left her guitar at Joey's, but if all they were doing was running through a few songs, she really didn't need it.

Grace sank down into one of the Adirondack chairs around the stone fire pit she suspected Gabe had made himself, as it was different from most of the pits she had seen running or walking by the other cabins.

She propped her feet up on the grey stone surrounding the fire pit and leaned back. The sky was dark, dotted with sparkling stars. Smoke grey wisps of clouds passed by a fat, full moon. Grace exhaled a breath, all tension gone for now, a blessed relief.

The screen door opened, and Gabe came outside, guitar case in hand.

"You look comfortable," he said, setting the case down on a chair before moving about the deck to gather firewood.

"I am," Grace said. "It must be this place. And the good food. And the company."

She caught his smile in the moonlight and smiled back, but when his eyes met hers, she looked away.

He was quiet as he got the fire going. Soon, yellow sparks drifted up and into the darkness.

"You ready?" Gabe asked. Grace noticed he had also carried his iPad out, probably to look up any songs they didn't know.

"You bet, what are we starting with?" Grace asked.

"You pick," he said, strumming a few bars on the guitar and humming along.

"How about we start with *Into the Mystic*?" she asked.

"Sure," he said, and started strumming the first few notes, nodding his head while he sang.

Grace joined in on the chorus. Their voices joined together and floated up with the sparks from the fire and disappeared into the night sky.

Chapter Eight

The next evening, Gabe stepped out of the shower to get ready to go to Snapper's. He stood in front of the mirror, towel wrapped around his waist. Drying his hair, he thought about what he would wear that evening. Usually, he would just throw on any old thing. Something like an old sweatshirt or t-shirt and jeans, Saints cap, and boots. Tonight was different. Tonight, Grace would be there. He wanted to look his best for her.

His thoughts turned to the night before. Even as relaxed as she had been signing, she still had that edge of anger in her voice and eyes. It had to have something to do with the band she left. Gabe wondered what would have happened that was so bad she'd walk away from it all. Gabe had no idea. Maybe she would trust him enough to tell him eventually. Maybe? There was no maybe. Gabe would do whatever it took to make her see that she could trust him.

Gabe reached out to grab some cologne from the vanity, and when he did, he saw his reflection. He wondered if she even noticed the changes he had made. How was he going to reach her when she was so far away?

He grabbed a newer pair of jeans and a green shirt that Carly had complimented him on the last time he wore it. He spiked his short hair with a little of that gooey stuff his hairdresser had pushed on him the last time he got it cut. After a final glance in the mirror, he was out the door.

• • • •

GRACE DID NOT FEEL like dressing up. She didn't even really feel like going out. She wanted to stay in her room in her pajamas and eat junk, listen to some good music on her iPod, or stare at something on TV. She still was not feeling sociable. She had too much on her mind. She would have to go to New Orleans soon and deal with the fallout from leaving the band. She needed to pack up her things at the apartment as well. At least she had this room at Joey's. She didn't have to worry about finding a place any time soon, or deposits. Other than a credit card and some student loans, she didn't have any real debt to worry about.

Grace stepped out of the shower and surveyed her traveling bag. Eventually, she was going to have to deal with that issue. She couldn't live out of it forever, and she was already getting tired of wearing the same old clothes. It had only been about a week, but she hadn't brought that many changes of clothes, and she hated doing laundry.

Finally deciding on a black baggy band shirt and jeans, she dressed quickly then paid some attention to her face. She applied a slight bit of eyeliner, mascara, and lip gloss. She tied her hair back into a ponytail. After a pat to Furby's head, she set out for Snapper's.

When she got there, Ryder, Joey, and Gabe were already there. They had taken their spot in the corner, and as usual there were two spots in the middle. One for her and one for Carly. As Grace had left Joey's, she had heard Carly moving around in her bedroom. She was arguing with her dog, Sammy, when Grace had walked by. Carly would be there later to join them.

The jukebox was playing as the karaoke deejay was setting up. A couple of the other regulars had a pool game going on. Grace said hello to the regulars she knew and went to meet the guys. Ryder had a pool stick in hand already. Either he had lost or was about to play next. She stopped and gave each guy a hug, then took the stool Ryder held out for her. One thing about her guys, they always treated her like a princess. If she was the princess, Carly was the queen. Especially considering that Joey was in love with her and had been in love with her for forever. One day, those two would figure it out. Grace wasn't getting in the middle of that. She loved them both too much.

"Any luck finding some more gigs?" Gabe asked.

"Not really," she said. "Everyone is booked right now. It's the season and no one wants to be without music." She frowned. "Maybe I can get some in a few weeks. I do have the ones coming up at the Wahoo."

Gabe said, "Something will turn up."

"It will."

She turned to Ryder. "Are you working in New Orleans again next week?"

"Yes, ma'am."

"Can I ride with you one day? I need to go by my apartment and get some things."

"It'll cost you," he said.

Grace rolled her eyes, "What will it cost me?"

He grinned, then grabbed her hand. "You gotta dance with me."

"Oh, all right. Jeesh," she said, smiling and let him twirl her out onto the dance floor.

• • • •

GABE WATCHED AS GRACE spun around the dance floor with Ryder. For a moment, she dropped her guard, her attitude, her anger, and was the Grace he remembered. As she danced, her long black hair swirled around her, her face beamed with happiness. Gabe smiled too. Maybe all she needed was to be home. Maybe she needed some distance away from New Orleans.

"What's going on with Grace?" Joey asked, coming to stand beside Gabe.

"I don't know," he said.

"I had hoped she might have said something to you. She's been spending so much time with you."

"She hasn't really said anything."

Joey sighed. "There's something going on with her. I just know it. It has to be something with Brent. Things seemed weird with them when we saw her in New Orleans a few weeks ago. She hasn't even spoken his name since she's been here. Asshole. I didn't like him in high school. I should probably just drive up there and whip his ass."

"You and me both. And don't forget Ryder."

"That's probably why she's not saying anything. Maybe she'll tell Carly. You know how Carly can be. We'll see if she can find out."

"That sounds good to me. Carly can be relentless at getting people to talk. I just hope she doesn't push too much. Grace may just clam up."

"True."

"Wouldn't hurt though."

"True."

They looked at each other, shrugged, and sipped their drinks.

· · · ·

GRACE RETURNED TO HER seat, endorphins pumping from the exertion on the dance floor. One Cajun dance should equal, like, three miles ran. All those spins and fast steps.

She took a big gulp of the glass Carly had sat in front of her earlier and closed her eyes, thirsty after that dance.

Ryder, who was now standing behind her, put his hands on her shoulder blades. Slowly, he began to knead the tension out.

"Damn, woman, you're tense," he said.

"I know," she said. "I don't know what's going on with me. Probably just the lack of a job thing."

"Maybe," he said.

"Any particular songs you want to sing tonight?" Grace asked Gabriel, changing the subject.

"How about I pick a few, and we just go with the flow."

"Sounds good to me." She and Gabe had done this many times before. She knew she could trust his song selections.

"Cool. Looks like he's about finished setting up now, so I'll just go write a few down."

"Awesome," she said.

Grace finished off her drink, and the bartender brought her a new one. Carly came in like the whirlwind she was, laughing, hugging everyone, teasing a friend here and there. With Carly's arrival came the first round of shots. If you were going to hang out with Carly, you were going to drink.

Gabe returned, and Ryder circled around after his pool game, and they grabbed their glasses and cheered to Grace and Gabe's return.

"It's going to be a good little crowd tonight," Carly said, nodding her blonde ponytail at the people beginning to gather in the small bar. "And Emily and Noah are coming as well. We should do a shot for that," Carly said, and ordered another round.

Grace inwardly groaned. This was not going to be pretty.

Carly downed another shot and reached for another karaoke song book. "I'm in an eighties mood tonight," she said, flipping through the pages.

"You're always in an eighties mood," Joey said.

Carly stuck her tongue out at him. "Are you singing?" she asked him.

"Hell no," he said.

"Then don't complain. It's like voting. If you don't sing, you can't complain," she said. "Grace, what are you thinking about singing tonight? You and Gabe doing a duet?" Carly smiled and nodded to Gabe.

Grace narrowed her eyes at Carly, knowing what was going in the wannabe matchmaker's head. "Yes, and no. Yes, we're singing a duet. No, we're not doing a duet."

Carly smiled and raised her eyebrows. "Is that what they're calling it these days?"

Grace swatted a hand toward the karaoke book. "Oh, go pick something," she grumbled, to which Carly only laughed.

"I will. I always start off karaoke night, gets the crowd going. But what to sing tonight." Carly went back to the selection book, and for that, Grace was grateful. She did not need Carly taking an interest in her love life.

"*Total Eclipse of the Heart*?" Carly read aloud. "No, that's too hard to sing, and I can't sing. Grace? You could sing that."

"I am not singing that cheesy crap." Grace laughed.

Joey high-fived her. "Thank you."

Carly glared at the both of them. "Fine. I'll keep looking. Oh, *Shadows of the Night*, Pat Benatar."

"I could do some Pat Benatar. I don't know about that one though," Grace said.

"I got it!" Carly said, grinning and scribbling on the slip of paper. She hopped up just as the DJ finished setting up his equipment. The DJ smiled, pulled up the song, and handed the mic to Carly.

Grace shook her head as Blondie's *One Way or Another* began to play. A perfect song for Carly—fun, bubbly, and not too hard to sing.

Carly began, and as she sang, started working the audience. She flirted and smiled. Winked a little. Grace smiled; she had chosen a song to get the party started and set the tone. Grace only hoped there would be no drunken versions of sad love songs later. That would be a definite buzz kill.

Carly teased her way through the song and had the crowd going. When the song ended, the small bar erupted in catcalls and applause. She grinned, did a full, deep bow, and handed the mic back to the DJ.

"Well, that's going to be a tough act to follow," Gabe said, laughing. "She's got those men all worked up. I'm almost scared to go now."

Grace laughed. "Right?"

Luckily, Gabe wasn't next. It was Allison, one of the regulars, and a teacher at a local high school. To the crowd's amusement, she began doing a rendition of Van Halen's *Hot for Teacher*.

"Well, I guess I can't let these ladies show me up," Grace said, writing down her song, then taking it to the karaoke table. When she came back, Emily and Noah had joined their group. They all greeted each other with hugs, then settled in, taking their familiar places around the bar.

Allison finished her song. Then it was Grace's turn, she had chosen Pat Benatar, but not *Shadows of the Night*. She chose Benatar's other fan favorite, *Hit Me With Your Best Shot*.

Not to be outdone, Grace worked the crowd just as she would have on Bourbon Street. Having performed this song many times, she didn't need to depend on the TV screen, so she walked through the crowd. She held the mic out to groups of single ladies and let them sing along.

She crossed over to the pool table where Ryder was standing with Gabe. She sang and ran her hand across Ryder's chest.

Playing along, he grabbed her, and they did a little dance during the bridge of the song. When the lyrics continued, she walked back through the bar and to the stage area where she finished the song.

She belted out the last notes and the song ended. She also gave a little bow before she left the stage, feeling the glow of performing.

As she walked back to the group, she was greeted with high fives, and Carly had brought them yet another round of shots.

"To Grace!" Carly said, raising her glass.

"To Grace!" the rest of them replied, and they all downed their shots.

"Okay, Grace, we're up next," Gabe said.

She followed Gabe to the small stage area set up. Grace grabbed the microphone Gabe offered her, and the familiar strains of a song they had sang many times together drifted through the bar. The last time she'd performed this song, she'd been with the band.

Brent.

"Bye sweetheart, it's been fun," his voice echoed in her mind.

Her insides froze, and she missed the next line. Gabe cut wide eyes at her, and she just shook her head, shrugged at him, then kept singing. She forced herself to finish the song.

When it was finished, she handed the mic to Gabe, turned, walked outside, and threw up.

· · · ·

GABE GAVE THE TWO MICS to Carly as the three watched a pale Grace walk out the door.

"Was it the shots?" Carly asked.

"I don't know," Gabe said.

Ryder, Joey, and Gabe looked at each other in confusion.

"I'll go check on her," Gabe said.

Outside, he found her leaning against Ryder's truck. Her head was tilted back, her eyes closed. In the moonlight, he could see tears on her cheeks. Grace didn't cry, but that was the second time in as many days he had seen tears.

"Grace?" he asked softly. He reached out for her arm.

"Don't touch me." She jerked away.

What the hell? He shoved his hands in his pockets. "Okay."

"What's wrong?" he asked.

"Get Ryder."

"Okay."

"Please."

Gabe re-entered the bar and glanced at Ryder, nodding his head to the door. Ryder sat his beer down and crossed over.

"What is it?" he asked.

"I don't know. She just told me to get you," Gabe said.

"Let me go see. Wait here. She won't want everyone out there making a fuss over her. That'll just piss her off," he said, and went outside.

· · · ·

"RYDER," GRACE SAID, seeing him come outside. She walked straight into arms that wrapped around her. He rested his chin on the top of her head.

"Take me home," she said.

Ryder leaned back and tipped her chin up to look her in the eye. "Now why would you want me to do that?"

She couldn't tell him why.

"If you want me to take you home, you're going to have to tell me why."

She would not tell him. She stuck her head in his chest, gripping the fabric of his shirt in her fists, unwilling to look up. She took a few deep breaths, a few inhales of his familiar cologne, his smell, and felt her panic disappear with each breath. He was her rock, and had been since her parents divorced, when Ben died, for every heartbreak and tear. He said nothing while they stood there, just held her close.

When her pulse slowed and her breathing regulated, she said, "Okay. Give me a sec and I'll come back in."

"You'd better. If you take off and walk home, I will drive down there and find you, and it won't be pretty." He smiled at her.

"I won't."

He kissed the top of her head. "Whatever it is, Grace. It will be okay. You will be okay."

"Promise?" she asked him.

"I promise." He gave her one more small squeeze and she stood there in the moonlight and watched him walk away.

• • • •

RYDER CAME BACK INTO the bar minus Grace.

"What's going on?" he, Joey, and Carly asked at the same time.

"I don't know. She won't tell me," Ryder said. "It's the weirdest thing. She has told me everything since we were twelve. Hell, some of the shit she told me I didn't even want to know, and she told me anyway." He shook his head. "You got me. It's your turn, Carly."

Noah interjected, "I wouldn't. She's not going to tell you."

Gabe looked at the war veteran, whose expression had taken the blank look that it sometimes did when he was battling the past.

"Noah's right," Carly said. "I'm not going to press her. We'll figure it out."

The side door opened, and Grace walked in and made a beeline for the bathroom. The group turned and acted like they hadn't been watching the door. Ryder went back to the pool table. Gabe turned to order a drink. He would not be going back to the karaoke table unless it was to sing a song by himself. Joey turned to talk to Carly about something.

"You okay?" he asked when Grace returned to her seat. Gabe noted the noticeable difference in her demeanor from earlier. She was not the twirling, smiling Grace on the dance floor. She sure wasn't the flirty performer. She was pale, hollow-eyed, withdrawn. Sad. He wanted to comfort her, to hold her, but was scared she would only push him away like she had outside.

"I think so," she said. "Must be stress or something."

"Maybe so," Gabe said.

"Gabe?" Grace asked. "Tell me all about Austin. I've never been there.

Gabe smiled, and began to tell her about all the local sights, the lights, the gorgeous lake just outside of town. "Gorgeous for a bike ride," he told her. "You should see it sometime."

"Maybe I will."

She was unusually quiet for the rest of the evening, even refusing to dance with Ryder, which had the cowboy frowning. Gabe sat there with her and just talked. He told her all about his roommates, Bennett and Nate, and Nate's damned snake that Gabe hated. The others settled into their routines, and Grace visibly relaxed when their attention was focused elsewhere. Gabe kept going, and he talked until Joey took her home.

Chapter Nine

G race woke up to a rainy, gray morning. The rain beat a rhythm on the metal roof that was both comforting and depressing. She looked down to see Furby lying on his back, one white, furry leg in the air like he was at a rock concert. If he could, he would probably have his index and pinky raised in the classic sign for "rock on."

Grace smiled slightly. He would not be happy when she went on a run without him, but he'd get over it. She patted him on the head and donned running clothes. She wished she had all of her clothes from her apartment so she could properly attire herself, but she would go with Ryder this week. She grabbed one of Joey's hats on the way out to keep her hair as dry as possible. Then she was off and running down the beach.

The air was wet and cold. The sun would finish rising, and soon the air would be almost unbearable with humidity. She would need to get out later and try to find some more gigs, or something to do. Grace did not do well with time off. She needed to be doing something. As Glinda would say, "Idle hands are the devil's playthings."

Grace smiled as she passed the Redbird. The lights were on, and Grace knew Glinda would be busy in the kitchen cooking breakfast. She'd pick something comforting this morning, like *pain perdu*, French toast, with different kinds of sauces and jellies to pour on top of the sweet gooey goodness. Grace thought of that fabulous strawberry sauce Glinda made from strawberries she grew and preserved herself. Maybe she'd pass by on her way back down the beach.

She continued running, taking in the dreary morning that reflected her mood. Never had she had a bubbly personality. In fact, generally, she sneered at those who were permanently perky. There was something just wrong with those people, Grace thought. Grace had never been one to be the clichéd depressed and angst-ridden musician either. She was just Grace. She got up every morning, faced the day, and tried to smile as often as she could.

She checked the distance on her running app, and satisfied she had run enough, she turned around. She was definitely going to stop by Glinda's later for breakfast. First, she would need to shower and change. Glinda wouldn't mind if she came in a sweaty but would get the wooden spoon out if Grace dripped water on those well-polished wood floors.

• • • •

GABE SMILED WHEN GRACE walked into the dining room of the inn. He had seen her running from his kitchen window when sipping his morning coffee. He didn't know how she did it. He barely functioned in the morning. The only things that got him out of bed that early in the morning were fishing and work. He tried to do as much of one as he did the other when he was home.

"Good morning," she said, hugging Glinda.

"Good morning, girl. How are you? You hungry? Go fix yourself a plate. So good to see you again."

"Morning," she said, sitting down next to Gabe after fixing her plate. "Good morning, Daniel."

"Good morning, pretty lady," he said. "You're becoming a welcome regular around our breakfast table."

She smiled. "It seems that way. What's new in the news this morning?"

"Well, there's an investigation going on in the St. Andrew Parish Sheriff's Department. Two of their deputies are under investigation after a traffic stop over the weekend. A young woman was taking a friend to work early in the morning. They pulled her over and made her do a sobriety field test. She was still in her pajamas, and she claims the officers made lewd and harassing comments."

"Ugh. Remind me not to drive through there any time soon," Grace said. "I'd probably be arrested. Jackasses."

"Yes. Seems to be getting worse with Mouton in charge. He's inept, and his officers know it. He turns a blind eye to their misbehavior so they think they can get away with anything."

"Well, luckily, there's no real reason to drive through that parish. Unless you're going to Biloxi, and most people just take the Interstate for that," Gabe said.

"True," Grace said.

"Maybe someone decent will run against him in the next election," Daniel said.

"If they can win. You know most of that parish is related to Jacque Mouton," Glinda replied. "But surely, people are getting sick and tired of all the corruption. I mean, come on. That poor girl."

"I guess we'll see," Daniel said.

Gabe sipped his coffee. He was more concerned about Grace than St. Andrew Parish politics. She still looked worn out, as if sleep was something constantly eluding her.

"Speaking of St. Andrew Parish, have you thought about that teaching job?" Daniel asked Grace.

"I don't want to teach," Grace replied.

Gabe looked at Grace. Her eyes were downcast. She was needlessly stirring her cup of coffee.

"I think Grace may be like me right now, just happy to be home." He knew it wasn't quite the truth, she was far from happy. A change of subject was what was needed.

Glinda smiled. "It's good to have both of you home. You'll be here for the cook-off next weekend. Carly told me she's changing it to a BBQ cook-off this year. You going to cook, Gabe?"

"I think I will. I do like to fire up a pit every now and then."

"You should. It's a good cause. I went to the scholarship presentation with Carly last year, and it was awesome to see."

"I'll think of something to cook, it will be fun. And maybe I can give Joey some competition."

"Great. Emily and I are getting together and making the sides. Daniel's already volunteered to judge. Maybe you and Grace can sing a couple of songs."

Gabe glanced over at Grace, who was still staring down at her cup.

"We'll see, Grandma."

Glinda looked from Gabe to Grace, then back to Gabe. She raised an eyebrow in question, to which Gabe simply shrugged.

Grace drained her coffee cup. "Glinda, it was wonderful as usual, but I'd better get home and do some job hunting. Carly should be up by now, and I can use her laptop."

"Of course, girl. Come back any time."

"I will." Grace stopped and hugged Glinda on the way out. "Thanks again."

Glinda's eyes followed Grace as she left. When the front door opened and closed, she turned to Gabe. "What is going on with her? Where's that spunk?"

He shook his head. "I have no clue, Grandma. No clue at all."

. . . .

GRACE LOOKED UP FROM the laptop. Her butt hurt and her shoulders ached. She had been sitting there for hours surfing the web, job hunting. Most of the open jobs were in New Orleans. That was not an option. Biloxi was the other closest choice, but she didn't want to move there.

She stood and stretched. She needed a walk to work the kinks out. She was definitely not used to so much sitting. She donned shoes and grabbed a drink.

The sun was beginning to set when she stopped close to the same spot she had chosen the night she'd gotten so drunk with Gabe. She wasn't doing that again. She had eaten today, though, at Glinda's and Joey had made a sandwich and set it beside her earlier. If she had wanted to, she could've gone and eaten at Emily's. If she didn't keep running in the mornings, she was going to gain twenty pounds just by moving home.

Moving? Was that what she was doing? Well, she didn't want to go back to New Orleans if she couldn't play music. She didn't want to wait tables or bartend. She had already been there and done that. She sighed.

She wanted something different.

Teaching would be different. Substituting wouldn't be a major commitment. She could leave if she didn't like it. No harm no foul. Just walk away. She didn't always play well with adults, but she liked kids. It couldn't be that difficult.

The job was also in the same parish as the Moutons. Brent's family. Brent was in New Orleans, but Denis wasn't, and he was just as bad as Brent.

To hell with it, that family had already taken her New Orleans job from her. They weren't taking another. She was applying. If she got it, she'd deal with the Moutons then.

She turned when she saw a shadow come up behind her. It was Gabe.

"Is this seat taken?" he asked, and he flopped down beside her.

"Now it is," she said, smiling.

"Whatcha thinking about?" he asked.

"I was thinking about that teaching job," she said.

"What about it?"

"I'm thinking about applying for it. I'd never get it," she said. "I don't have the experience. And I'm not certified."

"You never know," he said.

"I need something. I'm not going back to New Orleans right now. Other than to go get my stuff. And I need some income. Eventually, I need my own place. My own space. I can't do that on a gig once a week."

"True," Gabe said.

"So, I'll just apply and see what happens. Come up with Plan B."

"Good plan." He paused for a minute, as if thinking about what he was going to say. "You know, Grace. Our band has been talking about adding a female vocalist. That would be an option. You could come back to Austin with me."

Grace stared out at the sun setting. "I missed this," she said. "You never see a good sunset in town. Too many buildings. The water is so calm tonight, like glass."

She was quiet for a moment, then asked softly. "Gabe?"

"What, boo?" he asked.

"You're happy where you are?"

"Yes."

"I thought I could make a name for myself in New Orleans," she said.

"You still can, Grace. You just may have to find a different way."

She smiled. Gabe had always had faith in her. Years ago, he was one who had encouraged her to move to New Orleans when she had received the music scholarship. With all its bars and festivals, there were chances for her. She could work on a degree and still play. She had a better shot there than staying in Bon Chance. Despite its optimistic name, the opportunities for work were pretty limited, and a career in music was nonexistent. When Gabe had been awarded a scholarship to UT's film services department, he had gone to Austin. Bennett had gone along for the ride, and they had started a new band there.

Grace took a sip of her drink. She leaned back in the warm sand and rested her head on her arms. The stars were beginning to come out.

"Why does it always seem like the stars shine brighter here?" she said.

Gabe leaned back and lay down beside her. He looked up the sky.

"I don't know. Maybe it's because they don't have to compete with anything. They just get to shine," he said.

Grace smiled. "Maybe you're right." She took a deep breath and closed her eyes, and felt some anger disappear. For this moment, she would appreciate the sound of the water splashing against the shore, the company of a good friend, and the possibilities of tomorrow soothing her.

Chapter Ten

In New Orleans, Ryder followed Grace into the apartment. "You sure you don't want me to stick around and help? My errands can wait."

Grace's insides froze in fear. He could not see her room.

"No, I'm just going to pack what I need for now. I just need some more clothes and a few things. You go on."

He gave her a quick hug before walking out. "Call me if you need anything."

"You know I will."

Her smile faded as the door closed. Her stomach clenched. She did not want to be here. She wished she was anywhere but here. Why hadn't she just made Ryder a list and let him grab the things that she needed? Did she really need more clothes? She had made it this long. She blew out a long breath. Of course, she needed a few things. Especially if she was going to apply for that job in Pointe Shade. She couldn't wear a t-shirt and jeans or sweats if she got called for an interview. *If* she got called.

She threw the suitcase she had borrowed from Emily on the bare bed. The sheets she had pulled off the bed still lay in a jumbled mess in the corner of the room. She refused to look in that corner. She looked everywhere in the room but that corner.

"What did we do?" she remembered asking. "What did you do?"

"Bye, sweetheart. It was fun," Brent had said.

She looked at the corner then, at those sheets, and the wisp of a memory returned. Brent's cold hands on her face. She shuddered.

I should burn those sheets and the bed, she thought.

When she came to get the rest of her stuff, she was not bringing the bed with her. She'd toss it out of the window for a homeless person to find before she'd bring *that* home.

She tossed some clothes from the closet into the suitcase, some black slacks, the dressiest and most conservative shirts she owned. A couple of hooded jackets followed, then some more t-shirts and jeans.

She grabbed Furby's stuffed toys that laid in his bed on the floor and tucked them into a side pocket of the suitcase. He and Carly's dog had been going back and forth over her toys, and the tension between the two was mounting. Sammy wasn't one to share, and Furby liked harassing her.

She grabbed her writing journal from the bedside table and put that in the suitcase.

Her dresser was next—socks, underwear, etcetera. Bending down to open the drawer, her hand stilled on the handle when she saw the silver framed pictures of the band. Her stomach heaving, she bent over further in pain.

Hands on her knees, she exhaled a deep breath, and when the wave passed, she stood up.

In one sweeping motion, she knocked all the pictures off the dresser and onto the floor. Glass crashed against the wooden floor, splintering in shards all over the room.

Grace looked down at the mess, her breath ragged.

She stalked into the living room and grabbed a bottle of whiskey from the small bar she and her roommate kept stocked. She carried it back into the bedroom, twisted the top off, and took a big gulp. She gasped as it burned down her throat and her belly.

She took another gulp from the bottle and slid down the wall to the floor. She curled up, tucking her knees up to her chin.

Burn. She'd burn it all. A big, raging bonfire. She'd drink a glass of champagne while she watched. She'd watch the sparks float up and disappear into the dark night sky. Hell, she'd drink the entire bottle of champagne while the fire raged. She'd sit there until there was nothing left but ashes.

She was still crumpled on the floor when Ryder returned.

"Grace?" he said softly, seeing her curled up, whiskey bottle still in hand.

He looked from the mess of the sheets, the broken glass, to Grace. His dark eyes swept back to the sheets and he went still.

"Who?" His voice was a ragged whisper.

Grace looked down at the floor, refusing to look at him. She couldn't.

His boots echoed across the floor, along with the soft smash of glass underfoot.

She stared at his black cowboy boots.

He crouched down low and pulled the bottle of whisky out of her clenched hands. He took a long drink. With a heavy sigh, he sank down beside her. When his arm stretched out across her shoulders, she turned into his arms and sobbed.

• • • •

GABE WAS SITTING AT Snapper's having a drink, listening to music, and thinking about Grace when Ryder stormed in.

He sat at the bar beside Gabe, violence radiating from the normally frisky cowboy.

Gabe knew Grace had gone to New Orleans with Ryder to get her things. He hadn't heard from either of them. Judging by the dark look on his face, it hadn't gone well.

Carly, always perceptive, sat a beer and a shot of whiskey in front of him and looked at Gabe. Gabe raised an eyebrow, shrugged, and gestured for a shot himself. He sat there silently. You didn't poke the bull unless you wanted to get thrown.

Joey came in and walked straight to Ryder. "What the hell happened?"

Ryder turned to him, saying nothing but raising a dark eyebrow.

"Ryder, she's a mess. She's curled up in a ball in her bed. She isn't talking. This has gone on long enough, what is wrong with her?"

Ryder took a deep inhale of his cigarette. "I can't tell you."

"What the hell do you mean you can't tell me? I'm her brother!"

Ryder nodded at Carly, who poured another shot.

"Joey, do me a favor, go home and stay there. She doesn't need to be alone. I'm not going to tell you. It's not my story to tell."

Joey exhaled a breath. Frustrated, he ran his hand through his hair.

Carly, who had come around the bar after serving Ryder a shot, said, "He's right, Joey."

She laid her hand on Joey's shoulder. "Grace isn't going to talk unless she wants to, and it's not fair to expect Ryder to tell you and betray her confidence."

"I know. It's just tough. I have no clue what's going on or what to do."

Carly ran her hand over his arm. "I know. Why don't you go check on her? Text me and let me know how she is."

"I will." With a nod to Ryder and Gabe, he turned and left.

Ryder resumed drinking and smoking. Gabe sipped his own drink, staring at his phone. He considered texting Grace himself. He wanted to know if she was okay, especially after seeing Ryder and Joey's reactions.

"I know how you feel about her," Ryder said finally.

Gabe nodded.

"She's like my sister, you know. Just like Carly. I'd do anything in the world for either of them. To protect them." Ryder turned then and looked at Gabe, his eyes dark. "It's bad, Gabe. I can't tell you what it is. She needs us all."

He paused for a moment to take another drink, another drag off his cigarette. "If you're going to be there for her, though, be there. You can't do this half-assed. If you can't be what she needs, don't be there at all."

It was Gabe's turn to raise an eyebrow. "What makes you think I'm not serious?"

"Why haven't you said anything before? Why now?"

Gabriel took a slow sip of his drink before answering. "Because it's time. Because she needs me."

Ryder turned that dark gaze on him again, his eyes narrowed. Gabe met his gaze, unblinking.

Ryder nodded, then clasped his shoulder. "Come give me a hand. I have all of Grace's things and I need to unload them at Joey's."

• • • •

GABE WAS STANDING ON his deck, having a last drink, when he saw Grace sit down on the beach. She was in much the same position she was the night she got so drunk and threw the glass across the beach. Curled up. Dejected.

As if compelled, he went to her.

"Hey there," he said, sitting down. As he sat, he saw the glassy-eyed remnants of tears.

"Hi." She glanced at him, then stared back at the water.

"How are you doing?"

Her eyes flashed in the dark. "Why does everyone keep asking me that?'

Gabe decided to change the subject. "I went fishing with Noah today. Joey needed some fresh shrimp."

"Cool," she said.

"We caught a lot of shrimp today. More than Joey can use. We're going to have a boil tomorrow night. We haven't done that in a while. I think we're going to have it here on the beach. Best place to accommodate all of us."

"Cool."

Gabe was silent after that, having run out of things to say. Anything else would be babbling. He stared out at the waves. In the silence, all he could hear was the splash from the water as it hit land.

Minutes stretched out before Grace spoke.

"Gabe?" Her voice was soft and ragged.

"Yes, boo?"

"You still writing music?" she asked.

"Every now and then, when the mood hits me."

"I haven't written a line in months," she said. "I brought my journal home today. If I write the words, will you write the music?" she asked.

He put his arm around her then and hugged her close to his side. He felt her stiffen slightly and he pulled away. He heard her take a deep breath before she rested her head lightly on his shoulder. He could smell the citrusy smell of her shampoo. It was intoxicating. He took a deep breath but kept any reaction hidden, afraid he would frighten her.

"Of course, baby. Tell me when."

"Thank you."

Somehow, Gabe thought she was thanking him for more than the promise of writing a song together. They had written songs together when they were sixteen and planning on a music career that would take them to the big time.

She stretched out on the sand, her arms cradling her head. She stared up at the sky, still silent. Gabe laid down beside her, copying her pose.

He lay there with her silently in the moonlight, until her even breathing told him she had fallen asleep. He watched the moon inch its way across the night sky. Lost in thought, he wondered what Ryder had seen that was so bad. Judging by her responses to men, he was half afraid that he already knew.

Chapter Eleven

Yawning, Grace finished up the resume and hit *send*. She had applied for the teaching job in Pointe Shade. They wouldn't call. She'd keep looking for something else. Everyone would be nice and happy. Everyone but Grace.

She looked at her phone. It was time to meet everyone for the shrimp boil Gabe had told her about the night before. She didn't want to go. She wanted to curl up in bed and do nothing but stare at the TV until she fell asleep. She knew, though, that excuses and explanations would be harder than staying at home. Ryder had already sent her a text message making sure she was coming.

Ryder. He knew. He had sat there with her on the floor for God only knew how long. Seemed like hours but may have only been minutes. Then, silently, he had swept up the glass, ignoring the corner with the crumpled sheets. He had gone downstairs, come back with boxes. He packed everything he could and carried it to his truck.

Grace did not speak more than ten words on the hour and a half drive to Bon Chance. Staring out the window, she watched the world tick by in measures of trees and towns.

Ryder was silent as well, choosing to listen to music, chain smoke, and drive fast. He carried her suitcase in when they arrived at Joey's, and after a long look at her, he left. Grace had gone to her room. The four walls of her room felt like prison, though, so she had grabbed a few things and gone to the beach.

Gabe, she thought. How sweet he had been. He had sat there with her for most of the night. Even stretched out beside her for a while, but not touching her. She actually slept for a few hours. No nightmares. No restlessness. She'd like to say she felt better, but she didn't. She was still exhausted. Empty.

She looked in the mirror before leaving, thinking she should put some makeup on. Try to hide the smudges under her eyes. Add some color to the pale cheeks. Not even having the energy to do that, she tossed on a hoodie and shoes, and patted Furb on the head. "See ya later, buddy." He gave her a dramatic sigh and dropped his head on his furry white paws.

"Aw man, come on then." She laughed when he jumped down from the bed and did his little two-legged dance. She chased him in circles to get his leash on, then they went to join the others on the beach.

. . . .

WHEN SHE ARRIVED WHERE everyone had gathered, Grace saw Gabe clustered with Noah, Joey, and Ryder. They were busy fussing over the boiling pots. Well, Joey mostly. He was king here. He was working and trying to keep the other two out of the way. They weren't listening, though, despite Joey's looks and raised eyebrows. None of them noticed when she walked up.

It felt good to be home. Home was predictable. Home was safe.

"Grace!" Carly called when she saw her. Carly was reclining in a foldable lawn chair beside Emily. There was an empty seat beside her, and Grace sank down in it.

Carly reached into the cooler beside her and pulled out a beer.

"Have a drink, Grace. Relax," Carly said.

Grace slid the beer into the Snapper's coozie Carly offered. It was time to keep up appearances, so no one asked too many questions. "What's up?"

"Not much. Enjoying some sunshine and good company. It's a great day to be alive," Carly said.

"Hi, Em!" Grace said. "How are you? How is business?"

"It's going great, actually. Just picked up some holiday catering jobs in Lafayette. Hard to believe that the holidays are already just around the corner."

"That's awesome," Grace said.

"And, Carly, how's the book coming?" Grace asked. If Emily's dream was cooking, Carly's was writing. One day, Carly would publish a novel.

"It's coming. I haven't been dating, so not a lot of new material."

Carly was writing a second book on dating. Grace just shook her head. If Carly would open her eyes and see how much she loved Joey and how much Joey loved her, then Carly would have a whole different love story to write. Carly had titled her book *All I Want for Christmas is a Real Good Man*. She was in the process of trying to get it published, a process Grace was sure was about as easy getting signed with a record label. A long journey full of disappointment and rejection.

"Speaking of the holidays. It's almost time to start planning the Halloween party," Carly said. "The last one was a blast! And, Grace, you'll be here so you can dress up too! We'll have to go to New Orleans and do a girl's shopping trip for a costume!"

Grace felt the beer she had just sipped start to crawl back up her throat. She swallowed hard to keep it down. She was grateful when Daniel and Glinda walked up.

"Hello there!" they said as they sat their lawn chairs down in the little circle. Then, Gabe, Ryder, and Noah, finally run off by Joey, joined the circle as well.

Gabe sat his seat down on one side of Grace. After Ryder had kissed both Carly and Grace hello, he scooted in between the two. Ryder's dark eyes met hers for a moment, and he frowned, but soon hid it behind his crooked cowboy smile. Grace smiled, glad he understood her need for something normal.

"So, how's the job hunt going?" Daniel asked Grace.

"It's going. I sent that resume off to Pointe Shade today," she said.

"That's great," Daniel said. "*Bon chance*, pretty lady."

Yeah, right, Grace thought. She prayed she wouldn't get that job. Surely, there was something else out there. However, with the economy the way it was, that might be her only job opportunity here.

The group was quiet for a moment, which Carly never handled well, so she blurted out, "You know what we need?"

"What do we need?" Noah asked.

"We need some music out here," she said. "I can't believe we're not playing music already!"

"I got that," Noah said, and left.

"Awesome!" Carly said. "Great food, great company, great music!"

Grace smiled, Carly was known for her *joi de vivre*. And often, it was contagious. Carly was always so full of life, and happy, she brought others up with her. You never had a bad time when Carly was around. She wouldn't let you.

Noah backed his truck in and pulled the tail gate down. He had picked up Sadie and Oscar along the way, and they tore off across the beach, frolicking in the surf. He tuned in the radio and came back and sat down next to Emily. He reached for Emily's hand automatically. Grace smiled. At least someone got their happy ending.

Soon, Joey announced the food was ready, and they gathered around the foldable tables that had been set up earlier. Everyone filled their plates, grabbed a beer, and sat down to peel shrimp and munch on spicy boiled potatoes, corn, and sausage.

Grace let herself get caught up in this moment. She listened to the conversation and the laughter that always went along with good food and get-togethers. She laughed along with them as they relived past events and gave each other a hard time about this or that. Eventually, they started ribbing each other over who was going to win the cook-off the next day.

When the meal was finished and the mess put away, the sun was beginning to set across the water. Gabe disappeared to get his guitar, and Noah started a fire in the fire pit. Joey broke out the sticks and marshmallows. As the group melted marshmallows and made s'mores, Gabe sat and played the guitar. The light music blended with the snaps and pops of the fire.

Ryder took a seat beside her, and she leaned into the arm he wrapped round her. Warmed by firelight and friendship, Grace took a deep breath, closed her eyes, and felt a small piece of icy anger snap off and melt away.

Chapter Twelve

G race shuddered as Brent ran his cold fingers along her cheek. "Remember me, sweetheart?" he whispered in her ear. "I haven't forgotten you. And I'll be damned if I let you forget me. About this..."

Panic raced through Grace as she sat up in bed, heart racing, sweat beading her forehead. Her room was still dark, so it was either really late or really early. She looked over to her phone to see the time.

"Want to run, Furb?" she asked. The small dog jumped on the floor to dance in circles on his back legs. He barked once in response.

"Hush!" she fussed as Carly's dog barked in response. It was a reprimand for waking the old cranky dog.

"C'mon," she said, putting her shoes on. She hooked the leash on and carried him out the door in an effort to keep him quiet.

When they were out the door and out of earshot to wake sleeping dogs or people, she put him down, and they went to the beach. She let him off the leash and together they ran down the shoreline. The morning was cool, a signal that summer was definitely coming to an end and that fall would soon be there. The weather was supposed to be gorgeous today for the cook-off, and for that Grace was happy. Pretty weather meant a good turn-out, and that would be good for Benjamin's scholarship.

I haven't forgotten you...

Grace ran at full speed down the beach, ran until her lungs hurt and her knees ached. Only when Brent's voice stopped echoing in her head did she collapse on the beach, breathless. Finally numb, she pushed herself up off the cold sand and limped home.

. . . .

AFTER A SHOWER AND a nap, Grace walked up to the parking lot of Snapper's. Several cook-off contestants had already set up BBQ pits and tents. The smoky smell of burning coals floated on the air, combined with the sounds of music from the jukebox and the laughter and taunts from the people milling about and getting their food together.

The oilfield company men, in town for one last hurrah before the season ended, had all congregated and lined up along one side of the lot. The regulars who had chosen to participate claimed the other. So, not only was there the overall contest, there was also the regulars versus the tourists competition.

She passed Jay's tent first. "Hey Jay. Whatcha cooking?"

"Beer can chicken," he replied, holding up a can of Budweiser.

"You gonna have any left to shove up that chicken?" she asked, laughing.

"Oh, I'm sure Carly has plenty of Bud in there for me." He laughed.

"Oh, I'm sure."

Two other regulars, Walter and Red, had set up next to him. They had not started any kind of prep work other than to set up lawn chairs with a big red ice chest settled in between. They sat, beers in hand, their long legs stretched out.

"You guys cooking or what?" Grace asked.

"We're drinking."

"I see that. You going to actually cook anything?"

"Yep, shrimp kebobs. Seafood, quick cooking, less prep, more drinkin."

Grace shook her head. "You guys aren't right."

She kept walking until she got to the end. Joey, being his normal perfectionist self, had arrived early and his tent was closest to the bar. There was one tent and four pits. Joey, Noah, and Gabe would all be cooking that day. Ryder had been re-cruited to judge, as well as Daniel.

Kevin Douglas had joined them as well for the cook-off. Kevin had served with Noah in the Marine Corps. He had re-tired and returned home to his hometown of Point Shade. Un-like Noah, he still had the look of a military man. His hair was clipped short, his movements more precise. Noah's look was more relaxed, casual. You only saw the resemblance in their eyes, both on guard, and still haunted by things they had seen and could never forget.

Several chairs were set up. There would need to be because Carly, Emily, Grace, Glinda, and probably a few others would make that their home base for the day.

She was the only female to arrive so far. Carly would be in the bar overseeing things. Emily and Glinda would be along later with the sides for the feast. Grace had heard they were making an array of potato salad, rice dressing, pasta salads, and baked beans.

She took a seat in one of the chairs and watched as the guys started preparing their dishes. She laughed as they all ribbed one another. Joey was making smoked duck with a jalapeno cheese stuffing. Douglas and Noah were barbecuing ribs and competing against each other. Gabe was smoking a brisket. Ryder, seeing her arrival, left the group to meet her. His dark eyes scanned hers as if trying to ascertain what she was thinking, how she was. When she nodded and smiled, he kissed her forehead and took the seat next to her.

Grace surveyed the competitors across the lot again, wondering if they knew what they were getting into. She froze when she saw who had set up a tent across from them.

It was Denis Mouton and friends.

Brett's cousin.

What was that jackass doing here? Grace hoped he'd keep himself across the parking lot but knew better.

Carly walked up then. Blonde hair in a ponytail, big white sunglasses perched on her face. She had a pitcher of mimosas in one hand and plastic wine glasses in the other. Allison, the schoolteacher who had performed *Hot for Teacher*, walked up with her.

"Mimosa?" Carly asked Grace.

"Please."

Carly poured the drink and handed it to Grace. She then flopped down into the seat next to Grace. She kicked off her flip-flops and rested her feet on Ryder's lap.

"Thank God there won't be any drama at the cook-off this year," Carly said.

"Right?" Ryder said. "I'd hate to have to actually kick someone's ass this year."

"Sure you would." Carly laughed. "I've never seen you turn away from a good fight."

Ryder grinned. "Nope. Not me."

Grace knew they were referring to the spaghetti cook-off they had held the year before as a grand opening celebration for Snapper's. Emily's then husband had shown up, drunk and looking to cause a scene. He had come looking for Ryder after assuming Emily had a thing going with the cowboy. Emily had ended up going off on Eddie, throwing her ring at him and stalking off. Grace still wished she had been here for that.

"I wonder what Eddie would have done if you had actually walked off the porch?" Grace asked.

"He woulda got more than he bargained for, I assure you. After he called Em a whore, that was it. I was ready to whip his ass."

Grace sipped the mimosa and leaned back in the lawn chair, enjoying the feel of the warm sun on her face. A shadow crossed her face, and she opened her eyes to see that Gabe had finished up at his pit for the present and had joined them. She smiled when she saw him.

"Mimosa?" Carly asked him as she poured herself another.

Gabe held up a beer. "Nah, got a beer from Noah." He sat down in the seat next to Grace.

"What's up?" he asked her.

"Not much. Just relaxing." She bit back a yawn. "Still too early to do much."

"Bull-oney," he said. "I saw you running early this morning."

Grace's face blanched as she thought about the morning, about the dream she'd had of Brent. She cut her eyes over to the Mouton tent where they were milling about, laughing and drinking. Grace wondered if Carly had spoken too soon on the "no drama" comment. It might be Grace whipping some ass by the end of the day. As long as Mouton stayed on his side of the lot, things would be just fine.

"You okay?" Gabe asked.

She forced a smile. "I'm fine. How's the brisket coming?"

"It's looking good. I may give Joey a run for his money this year."

"Good for you," she said.

Noah and Douglas, finished up for the time being, joined them.

"I passed by the others on the way," Grace said. "Red and Walter crack me up. Shrimp they said. So they have more time to drink."

"That sounds about right."

The rest of the morning was filled with the guys getting up every now and then to check on pits, while the girls sat and had a few more mimosas and talked about the old days, men, and Carly's book on dating. Ryder wandered in and out of the group, making rounds, playing a game of pool here and there, but always resumed his spot between Carly and Grace.

As the day progressed, Grace felt herself relax. When Ryder came back, she, too, put her feet in his lap. His hand rested on her ankle, tapping with rhythm of the music that was piped through the speakers outside the bar.

Grace felt another shadow across her face, and she smiled automatically, thinking it was Gabe again. Her face fell when she saw Mouton's grey eyes leering at her. The sun behind him cast him in an evil glow.

"Well, hey there. If it isn't our little songbird?"

Grace slowly sat up from her reclining position and twisted her body to face his. "Well, if it isn't our neighborhood pig. Fitting to have you here for our BBQ. No one's tried to roast you?"

Grace heard Carly snicker behind her, but Grace didn't take her eyes off Mouton. Mouton shifted his eyes over to Carly, eyes narrowing when he saw her laugh.

Slowly, he turned back to Grace. "Funny girl, aren't you?"

"I prefer honest." Grace smiled.

"I was talking about you just this morning, by the way. Brent is in town from New Orleans this weekend. I told him about the cook-off, and he may stop in. Maybe you guys can revisit old times."

Grace felt the familiar bile rise at the mention of Brent's name. She made her face go blank, show no reaction despite her racing heart.

"Is that right?" Grace asked.

"Yes," Mouton said.

"Whatever," Grace said, shrugging.

Mouton, obviously disappointed with her lack of reaction, said, "Well then, we'll see you later." He nodded at the guys who had left their posts at their pits and stood behind the women. Beers in hand, they looked relaxed, but Grace knew better.

"We'll see you when they announce our names as the winners for the cook-off," Mouton said to the guys.

Joey smiled. "We will see about that, won't we?"

"Yes, we will," Mouton said, nodding his head to the ladies, then walking away.

The rest of them remained quiet as he left. "He's so gross!" Carly exclaimed. "Can we fix the cook-off? Please?"

Joey raised an eyebrow. "Are you saying I can't win fair and square?"

Carly laughed. "Of course not. How silly of me."

"Good."

Carly hopped up then. "Speaking of which, let me get things going with the judging."

Allison asked, "You need some help?"

"Nah, I got it. Emily and Glinda are coming up. They're going to help out." Carly handed the pitcher of mimosas to Allison. "You can make sure the mimosa glasses stay full."

"I can do that."

"Great," replied Carly as she flounced off across the parking lot and onto the porch. She grabbed a mic. "Judges and contestants, it's time for us to begin judging. Please bring your entries into the bar."

"You ready?" Allison asked, nodding toward Grace's empty glass.

"Yes, thanks."

Grace took a sip and leaned back in the chair again. "So, you teach, right?"

"Yep, I do."

"You like it?"

"I do."

"Is it hard?"

"It can be. But it can be rewarding as well. I love working with kids. Teenagers though. I don't think I could deal with the little ones."

"There's an opening in Pointe Shade."

"So I've heard."

"Gabe and Daniel think I should apply. I sent my resume off this morning."

"What do you think?" Allison asked.

"I don't know. It's something different, and a steady paycheck. And I do have a teaching degree."

"It's a sub position. If you don't like it, you don't have to go back. And I can help you with anything you need."

"I may take you up on that."

"Just one word of warning," Allison said.

"What's that?"

"Pointe Shade is very conservative, if you know what I mean."

"No, what do you mean?"

"They frown on drinking and sin. Think of that old movie *Footloose*." Allison laughed. "A friend of mine who taught there actually said she got called into the office for posting a picture of a beer on social media."

"You've got to be kidding me."

"Nope."

"Well, hell, they may fire me."

"Just keep a low profile and you'll be fine. The faculty isn't overly friendly anyway from what I hear."

"Good deal. I'll see what happens. They probably won't even hire me anyway."

"If they do, let me know if I can do anything to help."

"I will, thanks."

Carly interrupted then, announcing that it was time to announce the winners. Allison and Grace followed the others to the small area in front of the porch.

"Ladies and gentlemen, I want to thank you all for coming out. Again, the proceeds go to a good cause, the Benjamin Devereaux Scholarship Program. Last year, we were able to award a five hundred dollar a semester scholarship to a student from

Bon Chance High. This year, we're hoping to double that. And it's because all of you come out to events like this."

Carly raised the glass in her hand. "Before we announce the winner, let's all cheers to Ben, or Snapper. Miss you, my brother!"

"Cheers!" the crowd said as they raised their drinks to the sky.

"Now, let's see who the winners are." Carly looked down at the card in her hand.

"Honorable mention is the Moutons with pork tenderloin." Grace laughed when Carly rolled her eyes.

"Third place is Gabriel Angelle with brisket." Carly paused to let the crowd applaud.

"Second place is Noah Devereaux with ribs."

"First place this year is a tie, Joey Delchamp and Kevin Douglas. Joey Delchamp's entry was a pepper jack stuffed duck breast. Kevin Douglas's entry was ribs. Remember, folks, all entries can be sampled with the purchase of a wristband. We also have a silent auction with items donated by the Redbird Inn and Bon Chance Catering Company. The Devereaux family would again like to express our appreciation for all of you coming out and showing your support."

Carly smiled and raised her drink. "How about one more cheer for Ben and for the winners?"

The crowd cheered one more time, raising glasses to the sky.

Carly grinned. "Come on in y'all. Let's get this party started!"

Joey and Gabe high-fived each other and looked over to a glowering Denis Mouton, who had already started packing his things up to leave. Joey raised his beer in salute to the cop.

Gabe threw an arm over Grace's shoulder. "Let's go in. I'm ready for a celebratory drink."

Grace smiled. "Sounds like a plan."

After the winners were announced, the patrons of the bar with wristbands got to sample the goods from all the contestants, so a line had formed at the back of the bar where people usually danced.

The bar was fairly empty, so Grace and Gabe found their normal spot. Ryder was already there, as someone had challenged him to a pool game.

Gabe and Grace sipped their drinks and Carly brought a round of shots. Grace sat quietly, starting to feel the effects of the alcohol. At least she felt more relaxed, after her nerves had been shot after her run in with Denis Mouton. Her stomach still revolted at the thought of Brent coming later, but she'd cross that bridge if she had to. Who knew if that dickhead Mouton was just trying to get a reaction or what. She sipped the drink in her hand slowly and watched the guys play pool. Ryder was running the table. He had beaten Douglas, Gabe, and Joey, and was still playing.

Grace shook her head and sipped her drink. She was done with letting that douchebag pull her strings. Denis Mouton would not be ruining the day today.

"You ready to do some karaoke?" Gabe asked. The cook-off finished, the people who participated were either starting to pack up and go or staying to enjoy the party. The DJ who had been playing music in the background was now getting ready and setting up.

"Yes, let's sing for Ben. What do you want to sing tonight?" Grace asked.

"How about we start off with *Cheeseburger in Paradise*," Gabe said. "It was always one of Ben's favorites.

"Perfect. And fun," Grace said. Soon, Gabe was handing Grace the mic. They took their places on the dance floor where they could see the monitor for lyrics.

Grace looked out at the crowd, feeling exhilarated from singing, performing again. She felt her heart beat faster, in a good way. She met Gabe's eyes and smiled, and that faster beating heart of hers skipped one of those beats. She winked and was rewarded with a gorgeous blush.

Still smiling, she turned to look out at the crowd. Some had turned their seats to see them perform. Her gaze traveled through the bar.

Then stopped.

Brent Mouton smiled at her from the doorway.

Her heart pounded so loud she could hear it in her head. She forced herself to look at the screen, to read the lyrics. She would finish this song, she would not look back out at the crowd. Or at Gabe, who would see the panic in her eyes. She sang the lines automatically, barely hearing her own voice over the pounding in her head.

Out, must get out, repeated in her head like the chorus to a bad song.

What seemed like a lifetime later, the chorus faded and the song was over. Still not meeting Gabe's eyes, she handed him the mic and walked away, headed for the side door.

Brent stepped in front of her, halting her escape.

"You aren't going to say hi to an old friend?" he said, leering at her.

"You aren't a friend," Grace said.

"That's not what you thought that last night before you ran off. Left us high and dry. You think I'd let you forget that?"

Grace cut her eyes to the side and could see people watching, listening. She lowered her voice. "You bastard."

He started to reach out to touch her arm. Grace jumped and jerked away.

"Don't touch me."

"Again, that's not what you said the last time you saw me," he said, leaning in a little closer. "Do you want to know what else you said?"

Grace's palms itched with the desire to slap him across that smirk, across those lips that wouldn't shut up.

Grace resisted the urge for violence, but she could not stand there anymore. Shoving him aside, she ran out the door.

• • • •

GABRIEL WATCHED THE exchange between Brent and Grace. He watched her face change from panic, to anger, back to panic. Nothing that looked like this was a pleasant exchange. In no way was Grace happy to see him. It explained her hesitancy to talk about New Orleans, why she was here, and why she was so angry. Whatever had happened between them had been bad.

Gabe rushed to go outside to go to Grace.

Brent started to follow Grace out the door, only to be stopped by Ryder. Noah was behind them. Noah put a hand out to stop Gabe, shaking his head. "Watch him. I'll go to Grace. She'll be okay. I got this for now."

Gabe frowned, but nodded. This was not going to end well. Not well at all. He stepped closer to this potential powder keg, in case he needed to try to intervene. With Ryder, sometimes there was no reasoning with him.

Ryder stood in front of the guy and drawled, "I don't think she wants to talk to you."

"And?"

Gabe exhaled a breath, wanting to throttle the guy himself.

"That means you aren't going to talk to her."

"Who are you? Her keeper?"

"It doesn't matter who I am."

Brent shrugged. "You're right, it doesn't matter. She's just a cunt anyway."

Ryder flicked the cigarette he'd been smoking on the ground. "What did you say?"

"She's just a cunt."

Ryder's fist flew out, punching Brent right in the face. Brent stumbled back, hitting the wall. He shook his head a couple of times, then swung back at Ryder.

Ryder was ready. He dodged the punch, grabbed Brent by the collar, and shoved him against the wall, holding him there.

Gabriel held his breath, knowing that this was a Mouton from Pointe Shade, knowing this could have serious repercussions for Ryder if things went bad. But Ryder was Ryder and didn't give a damn.

Gabriel looked to Carly, who shrugged and said, "He won't listen to me."

Noah had followed Grace outside, and Joey would be no help at all. Joey looked like he was standing in line to whip Brent's ass next, if Gabe didn't get there first.

Kevin Douglas stepped up. He had probably talked down more than one angry Marine and had for Noah at the spaghetti cook-off the year before.

"Ryder," he said calmly, "I know you want to kick his ass. So do I."

Ryder's response was to push Brent against the wall again. "I am going to kick his ass. There's no want to about it."

"Yeah, but if you do, and those ignorant-ass Moutons decide to pitch a fit, you could have more trouble than they're worth."

"I don't give a damn," Ryder said. He released his choke hold on Brent, only to grab him by the shirt. He shoved him against the wall again, this time so hard it shook the neon lights and pictures on the wall.

"Okay, but do you have to do it in here? Carly will fuss forever over the blood on the floor. How about we escort this piece of shit outside."

Ryder released his hold on Brent's shirt, but in a lightning-fast movement, had Brent turned around, Ryder's arm around his neck.

The crowd that had gathered parted as Ryder pushed Brent through the bar. The clang of barstools hitting the floor rang out in the now silence of the bar. Not stopping to open the door, he let Brent's body push it open. Reaching the steps, he released his hold and Brent rolled down the steps and onto the parking lot. Ryder stormed down the stairs and stood above Brent's form lying in the gravel.

"You gonna get up or lay there all day? I'm not gonna kick a man while he's down, so I'll wait."

Brent scrambled backward across the parking lot.

"Go on, then," Ryder said, as he took a cigarette out of the pack and lit it. He drew on the cigarette while he watched Brent stand up slowly and limp to his car.

Carly joined him and handed Ryder a beer.

"As owner of this bar, you are not to step foot in this bar again," she said to Brent.

Carly and the others stood on the porch and watched him drive away. When the dust settled, she said, "So much for no drama this year."

She downed the rest of her drink.

• • • •

WALKING BEHIND RYDER'S truck and out of the view of passersby, she fought to control her breathing. Sweat beaded across her forehead and down the back of her neck. She gazed up at the sky, hoping to find relief in the softly setting sun, but found none. She closed her eyes.

She heard footsteps approach. "Go away," she said automatically.

"It's me, Noah." His voice was soft.

Grace's eyes popped open, and her head whipped around. "Noah?"

"Yes."

He walked up slowly, stopping to stand beside her as she leaned against Ryder's truck.

"You want to run, don't you?" he asked.

Run? Then realized that was exactly what she wanted to do. She wanted to run. Run down the beach. Run away.

"Can you do something for me?"

Unable to speak, she nodded.

"I want you to take a deep breath. While you do, tell yourself, 'Breathe in. Breathe out.'"

"Out loud?" she asked.

She heard him laugh lightly. "You can, or you can think it. Whatever you are comfortable with."

Grace closed her eyes again and leaned her head back. She focused on deep breaths, telling herself, *Breathe in, breathe out*, as she did. Slowly, she felt the vise that had taken up residence in her chest loosen. Her heart stopped racing, as did her thoughts and her almost undeniable desire to run away.

Noah stood there silently as she slowly came back down to normal.

"How did you know to do that?"

"I've had my own experiences with panic attacks."

"Panic attacks? I don't have panic attacks," she said.

Noah raised an eyebrow. "You sure about that? Racing heartbeat, can't breathe, want to run?"

"I've never had one before."

Grace realized then that it was a panic attack, and it was a result of her encounter with Brent.

Damn you, Brent, she thought. Would she ever be able to sing again?

"You okay to go back in? You can stay out here if you need, but I should probably go see what's going on. Do you want me to send someone out? Gabe?"

"I'll come in," she said, then stopped him, putting her hand on his arm. "Noah, thanks."

He smiled then. "No problem. And you know you can come talk to me anytime you need."

"I may do that," she said.

They went back in the bar only to find chaos. Emily was straightening barstools, patrons were either standing facing the door or outside. Grace watched as Noah walked over to Emily. He lowered his head to talk to her for a moment, then headed outside. Grace followed.

"What happened?" Grace asked when she got outside and saw Ryder, stiff with anger, standing with Gabe at the end of the porch. She could see soft tendrils of smoke from his cigarette waft up and float away.

"Let's go get a drink, and we'll talk about it," Carly said, crooking a head into the bar.

"Hold on for a moment," she told Carly. She walked over to the cowboy.

"Ryder?" she asked softly.

He looked straight ahead.

"You okay?" she asked.

He blew out a long stream of smoke and took a big swig of his beer, emptying it. He threw the empty bottle across the parking lot and into the grove of trees that surrounded the bar. Grace heard it shatter as it hit.

"It was him, wasn't it?"

Grace swallowed hard as pain knifed through her gut. Ryder still stared into space.

"Yes," she whispered, looking down. She saw Ryder's hands grip the railing of the wooden fence. His knuckles were white.

He turned to look at her then, his eyes stormy. He wrapped her in his arms then. "I'm so sorry this happened to you."

Grace rested her head on his chest, and he dropped his head down kissing her lightly on the top of hers. He held her for a long moment before letting go.

Gabe was next, wrapping his arms around her, only he didn't let go. "How about we go get a drink?" he asked. "I think we could use one. And a shot, for us and for Benjamin. It is his day after all."

Grace smiled. "Yes. For Ben."

Arm in arm, the three walked into the bar.

Chapter Thirteen

Grace wound her way through the crowded Bourbon Street bar. The song playing was her song, and she should be singing it. The crowd would not move to allow her to the stage. No vocals played, just the music, waiting for her to sing.

"Where do you think you're going?" Brent said, appearing out of the crowd suddenly and blocking her path.

"I'm going to sing."

"No, you aren't," he said.

Grace tried to move around him, but he reached out and grabbed her arm.

"You aren't going to sing. I won't allow it."

Grace pulled her arm back, trying to rid herself of his grip. It was too strong though. His fingers bit into the tender skin of her forearm.

She yanked her arm back, trying to break his hold.

"You aren't singing again!" Brent said. The background music rose to a crescendo and he laughed. Then he disappeared into the crowd.

• • • •

GASPING FOR AIR, GRACE opened her eyes. Concerned, Furby stuck his cold nose to her cheek. Grace put an arm around him and petted his furry head.

"Breathe in, breathe out," she said aloud, remembering what Noah had said.

The cook-off, Grace thought with a groan. After that fiasco, Grace had drunk entirely too much. She was still grateful that no one had asked too many questions. Sunday had been spent mostly in bed nursing a hangover and fending off texts from Ryder and Gabe.

She grabbed her phone off the nightstand to check the time.

Five a.m. On a Monday. Not long ago, she would have been finishing up a gig and heading home to get ready for a run before sleeping the day away to start the routine all over again.

She may not have a job yet, but she could still run. She threw on some running clothes, leashed Furby, and took off toward the beach.

When she and Furby got to the shoreline, Grace took off running. Furby ran beside her.

As she ran down the beach, the endorphins kicked in and she felt the stress melt away. If she didn't run, she would probably lose her mind. She still did not have a job. Nor did she have a job or a place to call her own. She needed her own space. Joey was great, but he was also her older brother. She needed some peace and quiet.

She needed a job. She needed a purpose. She was floating around with no anchor. And Grace had never liked to swim. Floating around aimlessly had always seemed pointless. Grace needed to move. To do something.

She would check the newspapers later to see what was available. Try Craigslist. Maybe someone in St. Andrews Parish was hiring. Too bad it was close to the off-season. She could easily find a waitressing job. Or bartending. Or something. Off-season was a bad time to look for employment. After Labor Day, jobs in Bon Chance were virtually non-existent. Singing or playing was out of the question for now. She might try a few practice runs, but as things were now, she couldn't perform if she had to puke or run out the door every half hour.

So, she'd have to find something soon.

On her way back home, she saw Noah. He was standing at the edge of the surf, throwing a stick into the waves. Sadie, the German Shepherd, was the only one running into the water. Oscar, the mutant Boston Terrier with the big head, stood on dry land and would play tug of war with it when the other dog ran back with the stick.

"Mornin'," Noah said with a nod as Grace approached.

"Morning."

"How you doing this morning?"

"I'm okay," she said.

Noah narrowed dark eyes at her. "You sure?"

"I'm sure."

He stared at her for a moment, silent, as if unsure if he wanted to say what was on his mind. He finally exhaled a deep breath and looked her in the eye.

"You know, Grace, I've seen you out here in the morning. Sometimes you run as if the hounds of hell are after you, you go until you can't run anymore."

He stopped again and looked out to the horizon. "There are some things you just can't outrun."

Grace's eyes burned. Tears threatening, she looked away.

"You don't have to say anything. You don't have to talk at all," Noah said. He reached into the pocket of his hooded jacket and pulled out a set of keys. He twisted a small key off the chain and handed it to her.

"This is a key to my houseboat. I want you to have it. I did a lot of thinking there." He reached out to hand it to her, stopping when Grace went to grab it.

"You can go whenever you like, whenever you feel the need to escape." He smiled slightly. "I do like to have a cup of coffee on the deck in the mornings after my run. I would like it if you would join me. Starting tomorrow."

A shadow passed over his face, and he looked away. "I think it might do both of us some good."

Grace chewed her bottom lip. The key felt warm in her palm. "Thanks, Noah. I will take you up on that."

Noah smiled. "Good." He nodded at the group of dogs who had grown bored and were now wrestling each other in the sand. "I'd better get these mutts back to the house and hosed off."

He whistled and the dogs sprang to attention. Even crazy, anti-social Furby, who had been barking at the dogs off and on, stopped by Grace's side and sat.

"I'll see you for coffee in the morning?" Noah asked.

Grace smiled. "Yes. You will."

With that, Noah and crew walked off, leaving Grace on the beach alone with Furby. Grace opened her palm and looked at the key. The early morning sunlight glinted off the gold key.

An escape. She looked across the horizon where she could see the houseboat bobbing slowly off the pier.

Maybe that was exactly what she needed. No Gabe. No Ryder. No Joey. As much as she loved them, their questioning glances were almost too much. She didn't have any answers for them. She didn't have any answers for herself.

Maybe now she could find the answers and peace she needed.

• • • •

ON THE WALK BACK TO Joey's, Grace felt the phone on her hip vibrate. Grabbing it, she looked down, expecting to see Gabe asking where she was for breakfast. She was surprised with a number she didn't recognize. She let it go to voicemail. When the phone vibrated again, she clicked on her voice mail.

"Shit!" Grace said as she listened to the message. "Shit! Shit! Shit!"

"Ms. Delchamp. This is Troy Comeaux at Point Shade High School. I received your resume this morning. I'd like to schedule an interview with you."

What was she going to do? She didn't want the job! She had only sent her resume to get everyone off her back. She just wouldn't call him back. Grace shrugged her shoulders.

That was it. She just wouldn't call him back. Then she thought of the teacher's salary she had seen posted on the parish's website.

She did need a job.

That was a lot of money. Even more money than she was making singing on Bourbon. She could get her own place with that. She could save some until she figured out what she wanted to do next. She might even buy a car.

She was just kidding herself anyway. They weren't going to hire her. She wasn't qualified. She had a snowball's chance in hell of getting that job. Maybe they would have a clerical job come open or something.

Sighing, she clicked through and found the number on caller ID and pressed the button.

. . . .

LATER THAT AFTERNOON, Grace walked into Snapper's, already feeling foul.

"I have an interview tomorrow," she told Gabe as she sat down.

"Oh really? That's great," he said. "Where at?"

"Point Shade High School. That sub position."

"Awesome," he said.

"I'm not going to get it," she said.

"Why not?"

"I'm not a teacher. And I don't want the job anyway," Grace said.

"Well, it will work until you can figure out what you do want."

"They aren't going to hire me," she argued.

"You never know. I think we should toast to the interview," he said, holding out his glass.

"I. Don't. Want. This. Job," she said, glaring at him.

He smiled back. "Well, okay, then. Let's just toast to new possibilities," he said.

She smiled then. "I can toast to that. Hopefully, I'll have some. Speaking of which, I have my writing notebook. When do you want to get together and do some writing?"

"Whenever you want. We can start tomorrow after your interview, if you'd like. Since we're not going to be celebrating your employment, Miss I'm Not Going to Get the Job Anyway."

"I'm not. They probably just have to interview a certain amount of people."

"You never know."

"Let's toast and talk about something else," Grace said.

"Talk about what?" Ryder asked as he walked up. He hugged Grace, shook hands with Gabe, and had a seat beside Grace.

"The job I'm not going to get."

"You have an interview?"

"Yeah, but I'm not going. I changed my mind," Grace said. "I'm not going to waste anyone's time."

"And why not?"

"I don't want to. I don't want the job."

"Grace, it's a good opportunity for you. It's only temporary. If you don't like it, you don't have to go back," Gabriel said.

"So why go in the first place? I'm not going to get the job."

"Then what's the harm?" Gabe asked.

"Why should I?"

"Grace. Go to that interview," Ryder demanded.

"I'm not going."

"Listen, Grace. Go."

"Nope."

"You're being an idiot."

"You're being an ass."

"And?" Ryder flashed her a smile. "What's new?"

"Just go. What other option do you have right now? You cancelled your gigs. You need a job. Steady income. Go," Gabe, always the voice of reason, said.

"Fine," she said. "I'll go, but I won't accept it if they offer."

"You're too smart for that." Gabe ruffled her hair.

"You'll do what you need to do. You always do," Ryder said. "And on a side note, you are going to meet Noah in the morning for coffee."

Grace raised an eyebrow. "You talked to Noah?"

"He talked to me about it last night. And I agreed that it was a good idea."

"I'm going to go. He said it would help him too."

"I have no doubt," he said, and patted her leg. "Now, let me go whip Gabe's ass on the pool table."

"You do that," Grace said before grinning, not at what Ryder said but at Gabe rolling his eyes behind Ryder's back.

She leaned back in the barstool and propped her knees on the ledge of the bar. She would meet Noah for coffee. She would go to that interview. They wouldn't hire her, but it felt like a step in the right direction. A step Grace needed to get her life back together.

Chapter Fourteen

The sun was a yellow dot in the pink morning sky as Grace ran down the deserted beach. On the horizon, she saw Noah's houseboat bobbing slowly by the pier. A lone pelican rested on a wooden pylon jutting out of the water. She slowed to a walk as she approached, her hand going into the pocket of her hooded sweater to find the key.

Maybe Noah was right.

Her footsteps echoed across the old wooden pier as she walked to the boat. She passed through the small metal gate and onto the deck. She felt like an intruder, and even though she had the key, she chose not to use it. Going instead around the deck to the front of the boat where a pair of white wooden rocking chairs sat.

She settled into one of the chairs and let the movement of the chairs and the water lull her into a sense of serenity she hadn't felt in days. From where she sat, she could see the sun slowly continuing its ascent into the sky. Pinks, yellows, and blues stretched out as far as she could see.

Grace leaned back in the chair, closing her eyes. Random words and phrases began to string together with a melody.

She hadn't written an original song in ages. It was time. She would bring her music journal and leave it here somewhere safe so she could write down ideas.

The sound of footsteps alerted her to Noah's presence before she saw the dogs run across the beach, free at last to romp in the surf.

The boat creaked as Noah entered the cabin, Grace assumed, to make coffee. Soon, the sliding glass doors opened.

"Mornin'," Noah said, and Grace felt his dark eyes on her, assessing her. He set a cup of coffee down beside her. "I can get cream and sugar if you need."

"I'm good," she said.

"Nightmares?" he asked.

Grace nodded, and he exhaled a breath as he settled into his chair. She was struck again by the changes he had made since the year before. Not as skinny, not as withdrawn, he seemed to have put his demons to rest. For the time being, at least.

Steam rose from his coffee in the cool morning air as he took a sip. He leaned back in the chair, looking out at the horizon, his thoughts farther away than Grace could ever know.

"Grace, I'm not going to ask you what happened. That's for you to tell when you are ready. I know that Ryder knows, and that's good enough for me. I just don't want you to think these morning talks will be about me trying to get you to talk. Hell, some mornings I may not even want to talk at all. Sometimes just sitting can do wonders for the mind."

"I don't think I've ever really just sat and done nothing," Grace said. She felt like she was sometimes constantly in motion. Music, practice, running, social life, she was always busy unless she was sleeping. And she wasn't even doing that too much these days.

"Maybe it's time you started," he said, taking another long sip of coffee. He was quiet again as he stared straight ahead. Grace said nothing as well, not sure of what to say.

He exhaled a deep breath. "When I got back from Iraq, I had nightmares. A lot. I got to the point where I dreaded sleep. I still have the nightmares every now and then. I probably always will. At least Em seems to have gotten used to them. I think I scared the shit out of her a few times."

"I'm sure she understands," Grace said.

"I'm sure she thinks she does," Noah said, "and I love her for it. But she can't. No one can who hasn't been there."

"Do you ever talk to her about it?" Grace asked.

"Not really. I've never talked about it with anyone, until now."

"Why me?" Grace had to know. Why talk to her rather than Emily?

"Like I said when I handed you the key, I think this can help both of us. Emily knows I need to talk and that you do too." He drained his coffee cup.

"Want another?" he asked her.

"Yes." She handed him the cup, and he disappeared back into the cabin.

"So, I hear you have an interview today," he said when he reappeared with two mugs.

"Yes, I guess I'm going," Grace said. "I still don't know if I want the job."

"I understand," he said.

"You do?"

"I do. And we can talk about that later. You can tell me all about it tomorrow morning. If you want to."

Grace nodded and smiled. She sipped her coffee and looked out at the calm water. Noah was right about one thing. These talks might just be good for them both.

• • • •

WALKING INTO THE DOUBLE doors of the high school, Grace tugged on the one dress shirt she owned, feeling like she was wearing a Halloween costume that didn't fit quite right.

"Ms. Delchamp, thank you for coming in," the principal said as she walked into his office. He motioned to the seat across from his desk.

Great, the principal's office, Grace thought. *Like I didn't sit here enough in high school.*

"Please, have a seat."

Grace sat in the chair and resisted the urge to cross her arms and glare.

She. Did. Not. Want. This. Job.

She didn't want to be here, but that was okay. She wasn't going to get the job anyway.

She mentally shrugged her shoulders and met the principal's eyes.

"So, Ms. Delchamp, what we have here is an English teaching position, eleventh graders. Your resume states you have a degree in music education. Why did you never pursue a career in education?"

Because I don't want to teach, she thought. She paused while she thought of a more acceptable response. "I've always loved to play music. I wanted to see what I could do before I settled down into a career. So, I moved to New Orleans to play there."

"And you're coming back because...?"

Her stomach rolled, and she fought to keep her face impassive. "It wasn't working out."

"Okay, let me tell you a little bit about this position. It is a substitute position for the remainder of the year. Due to an unfortunate series of events, the teacher we had will not be returning."

That's one way to put it, Grace thought. The dude lost his mind and ran around half naked in a city park wearing lipstick and panties.

"I understand," Grace said.

"So, tell me about yourself," he said.

"I'm a musician. I've been writing and playing music since, well, since as long as I can remember," she said.

"Why teach?" he asked.

"I had hoped to share my love for music with students eventually."

"What do you know about teaching English?" he asked.

"Very little," Grace admitted. She wasn't going to try to impress him. She didn't want this job, and so far, it looked like she wasn't going to get it. She relaxed and waited for him to say, "Thank you for coming in, we'll call you."

"Basically, you just teach them the curriculum set forth by the state. Teach them reading skills and how to speak and write grammatically," he said.

"That sounds like something I could do," Grace said, playing along.

"If I asked you what your main fault was, what would you say?" he asked.

"I'm stubborn," she said. There, that should do it. Nail that coffin shut.

He smiled at her. "That's not always a bad thing. I'm going to be honest here, Ms. Delchamp. I like you and I need to fill this position. It being during the year, it's been rather difficult to find someone with the qualifications, especially here in a smaller town. If I offered you this position today, would you take it?"

He's going to offer me this job, she thought. *Damn, damn, damn.* What would she say? What could she say? Ryder was right, she needed some income.

"I would take it."

"Well, then, it looks like you're hired." He reached forward, his hand extended. "Welcome to Pointe Shade High School. If you have time, I can give you the grand tour."

Grace nodded, speechless.

Damn. Damn. Damn.

She was still cursing as he led her through the now quiet halls of the school. He took her through the small but modern library first, as it was adjacent to the office area.

"We have all the new technology that the students would need to be prepared for college and life after. What classes we don't offer here, we have online options for."

He led her out of the library and down the hall, stopping at a room and opening the door.

Grace's mouth fell open when he clicked the light on.

"It's a bit of a mess," the principal said.

"A bit?" Grace asked. Grace wondered if the room was the remnants of a hurricane, or if someone really could work in what could be described as chaos. Books of all types littered the floor: textbooks, novels, workbooks. You name it and they were on the floor. The bookcases spilled over too, shoved full of books and notebooks that looked like they had been housed there since the school was built. Student work was plastered all over the walls. Some posters had yellowed and faded.

"Mr. Thibodeaux left in a hurry, as you may know, and has not yet come to clean up his belongings. A janitor will be in later today to bring some kind of order to this, so don't think that you're going to be responsible for the organization and preparation of this room."

"Thank God," Grace said under her breath. The principal chuckled.

"How about you plan on starting next Monday? That will give you time to prepare, and we can get this room in proper order. Would you like to take any materials with you?"

Grace stepped over piles of books and folders to cross over to the teacher's desk that was also piled high with stuff. She grabbed what looked like a teacher's manual. Looking again, she saw a copy of *The Great Gatsby*. She grabbed that too.

"I think this is enough to get me started."

"Great. Is there anything in this room you see that you'd like to keep?"

She scanned the room one more time. "Nothing. Nothing at all. Keep the books, that's it."

"A clean slate," said Mr. Comeaux. "I like that."

"Me too," Grace said. "Me too."

Mr. Comeaux shook her hand at the main intersection of the hall after the interview. "Well, Ms. Delchamp, we'll look forward to seeing you Monday, then. Please call me if you have any questions at all between now and then."

"I will," Grace promised. "See you Monday."

He nodded, and Grace walked away, a tight knot of anxiety tangled in her stomach.

What the hell was she going to do now?

• • • •

A FEW MILES DOWN THE road, she pulled Joey's Jeep over on the side of the road. She had borrowed it, thinking that pulling up on a Harley would not make the best first impression. She called Ryder.

"Ryder? I got the job. I start Monday," she said. "Now what the hell do I do?"

"Well, you go to work," he said, and laughed.

"And? I don't know anything about teaching English."

"You speak it, don't ya?" he asked.

"Most of the time."

"Well, then, what's the problem?"

"I don't know anything about it. Teaching reading, books?"

"You read, don't you?"

"Yes."

"You write music?"

"Yes."

"Okay. You read, you speak English. You can write. The rest you can figure out."

"It's not that easy!"

He sighed. "It's not easy because you're making it more complicated than it is. Use what you know and go from there. You can figure out the rest."

"I'm going to call him back. Tell him I changed my mind."

"Don't you dare," he said. "Don't be stupid."

"Fine."

"Now, come on back here. Let's have a drink to celebrate."

"I don't want to celebrate."

"Get your ass over to Snapper's tonight. I'll be there after I get home from work. Call Gabe and have him come meet you."

"Fine."

Ryder hung up, and Grace sat there on the side of the road staring at the phone, wondering what the hell she had gotten herself into.

"I guess I'll find out," she said, putting the car into drive and heading back to Bon Chance.

• • • •

GABE WAS ALREADY AT Snapper's. He had finished the work Glinda had needed done and was feeling restless. He had gotten the text from Grace earlier telling him about the job, asking him to meet him at Snapper's. Like he'd be anywhere else. He'd sip his drink. Then look at the door. Then sip his drink. Then, Grace walked in.

His body reacted when he saw her. His heartbeat sped up. His hands itched to touch her.

She smiled when she saw him, and his pulse kicked up a notch. He resisted the urge to rub his palms against his jeans like a nervous teenager. He smiled back and pulled out the barstool next to him. Carly was there already, placing a shot and a drink down on the bar in front of where Grace would sit.

Gabe inhaled the clean, citrusy scent of her shampoo as she hugged him before she sat. She looked gorgeous in her simple jeans and t-shirt, minimal makeup, and ponytail. She still had those smudges under her eyes, but maybe soon those would fade away.

Carly brought a round of shots. "Congrats on the job!"

"Thanks, I guess," Grace said after they all they all set the shot glasses down on the bar. "I don't know what the hell I'm going to do, but, oh well."

"I sent Allison a text. She's going to come in later, so we can ask her," Carly said.

"That would be awesome," Grace said, then proceeded to fill them in on the interview and that disaster of a classroom.

"It really looked that bad?" Gabe asked.

"I should have pulled out my phone and taken a picture," Grace said. "I think I was too shocked."

"Well, they'll get it all together for you. And it's not like you have to dive in tomorrow. You have some time. "

'That's true," Grace said.

"Well, what's on your agenda for the rest of the night?" Gabe asked.

"Ryder's coming in a little while. He's at home changing. So is Joey. I guess I'll be hanging out here, unless something changes."

"We could do a bar crawl," Carly said. "Head over to the Wahoo or 31. See what's going on."

Grace's stomach revolted at the thought of going to 31, where the Pointe Shade police made regular appearances. After the cook-off, she hoped to never see any Mouton again.

"Or not," Carly said, seeing her reaction. "We can stay here. Less trouble."

"Yeah," Gabe agreed. "We can just hang out here, play some jukebox. Some pool. Just chill."

"Sounds like a plan to me," Grace said. "I need some chill in my life right now."

Carly left to tend to some customers, and Grace turned to Gabe. "I thought about writing some music this morning."

"Is that right?"

"Yeah, I was at Noah's, looking out at the water, and some lines, some music, came to me."

"Awesome."

"Yeah, it felt good," she said, smiling.

"Well, we'll just have to get our guitars out and see what we can come up with," Gabe said. "You know, Grace, if you wanted, you could come play with us in Austin."

Her smile disappeared. "I can't."

Damnit, Gabe thought. He'd messed that up, hadn't he? What to do now? And why had she been at Noah's anyway? So many questions with Grace. He just wished she trusted him enough to give him some answers.

"Well, how about we play some music later on the jukebox? May get some inspiration?"

"Sounds good to me."

Ryder made his appearance then, stepping up on the ledge of the bar to lean over and kiss Carly. He grabbed his beer from her, then hugged Grace. Gabe noticed that he held her out at arm's length for a moment to look her over. He tipped his head in a slight nod before pulling out a stool and sitting down with them. He reclined back, resting his boot on the bottom rung of Grace's barstool. He lit a cigarette and blew out a stream of smoke.

"Play some pool?" he asked Gabe.

"Sure. Set 'em up."

"I will, after this beer. Work made me thirsty." He grinned.

"How you doing?" Ryder asked Grace. "Dance later?"

"I think you could talk me into it," she said.

"Good." He downed the rest of the beer.

"Let's get this party started." He took off his cowboy hat and shoved it on Grace's head. "For our Grace."

Soon, the party was joined by Noah, Joey, Kevin Douglas, and finally, Allison. Carly's shift ended, and she switched sides of the bar. Everyone was there but Emily, who had a catering gig that evening. As the evening progressed, Gabe was glad to see Grace relax, laugh, and be her old self. He pulled out a five-dollar bill and went to the jukebox to play some music. He played a few songs he knew she liked, some songs they had played that night on his porch, and a couple of other songs just because.

He smiled when she sat beside him and sang along as Van Morrison's *Into the Mystic* played. If anyone had a "gypsy soul," it was Grace. It felt good to sit there with her and sing a few songs. It felt like home. He hoped he could get her to perform with him again, even come to Austin.

"Oh my god!" Grace exclaimed when *Against All Odds* started playing. "We sang this for the prom!"

"Yes, we did," he said, nodding.

"Oh my gosh! I loved this song! Joey, come dance with me!" Carly said, grabbing Joey and dragging him to the dance floor. Gabe shook his head, almost feeling sorry for him. Almost. Knowing how Joey felt about Carly, Gabe suspected he enjoyed the moments he got to be close to her. Speaking of being close...

"Grace, you feel like a dance?" Gabe asked. She had danced with Ryder a few times already, but it was the complicated Cajun dancing they always did together. Nothing slow.

Indecision showed on her face, and Gabe thought for a moment that she was going to say no. She took a deep breath, looked him in the eye, and surprised him by saying, "Sure."

He led her onto the dance floor, his hand on her arm, not too tight. He knew how jumpy she'd been lately, and he didn't want her to feel uncomfortable. He took her into his arms, close but not too close. Close enough that he could smell her light, citrusy perfume.

She was a little stiff at first, even missing a step once, but as the song played, she relaxed. So did Gabe, who hadn't even realized how nervous he was over this simple dance. He resisted the urge to bend down and kiss the top of her head. *Baby steps*, he thought. *Baby steps*.

The song was over much too soon, and they resumed their spots at the bar. He didn't ask her to dance again. He wanted to but didn't want to press her. He still didn't know what was going on with her, but he did know one thing. He wasn't giving up.

Chapter Fifteen

The sun was rising above the water when Grace took a seat in the rocking chair on Noah's boat. The morning was quiet, the only sound the slap of water hitting the sides of the houseboat. Her writing journal sat open on her lap, but she hadn't written anything yet. For now, she was content to just sit and enjoy the early morning.

She stretched, feeling better than she had in days after a night of sleep without nightmares. Looking down at the journal again, she thought of Gabriel. It had felt good to dance with him. It had been awkward at first, but he was so easy to be with. It had felt almost natural to relax and sway along to the music with him. Almost. It wasn't like dancing with Ryder. Gabriel wanted more from her than just a dance. She could see the attraction in his eyes. He was Gabriel, a strange mixture of the known and unknown. Had that attraction always been there? Had she missed it?

She heard Noah walk up. He would make some coffee, then come out. She closed the journal and placed it on the table between the two rocking chairs.

It wasn't long before he came out with two mugs in hand. He had the *Semper Fi* mug and had handed Grace the *Life's a Beach* mug. She took a sip as he settled into the chair next to her.

Like the day before, he rocked silently, taking in the view before speaking. Grace wondered if he was thinking of what to say, or if he was just taking his own moment to enjoy the view and the quiet.

Nothing but pastel blues and pinks, a row of rocks jutted out a few yards out that various birds used to rest on before taking flight and dipping down to catch their morning meal.

"How'd you sleep last night?" he asked after a few sips of coffee.

"No nightmares," she said.

"Good." He nodded. "I didn't have any either. I think that's a good thing. How are you feeling about the new job?"

"Nervous."

"Something new is always unnerving. You can do this though, remember. Breathe in, breathe out."

"I can do that."

"I know you can."

Noah got up once to refill their cups. Time clicked by as they rocked in their chairs and watched the sun finish rising.

• • • •

LATER, GRACE WALKED down the beach with Furby. It was warm, the sun bright in the almost cloudless sky. A great day for a bike ride, she thought. If only her gas gauge was working right. She longed to feel the freedom of the open road. Feeling the wind, smelling fresh cut grass, nothing between her and the scenery.

As she passed by the Redbird Inn, she saw Gabe fishing, out enjoying the sunshine as well.

"What's up?" she asked as she approached.

"Nothing much," he said. "Killing time with some fishing. I'm not used to all this free time."

"Me either," she agreed. "I was thinking that it would be a great day for a motorcycle trip."

He looked up and nodded. "I agree. Don't you have a bike?"

"I do, but it needs some work done. It left me on the side of the road on my way here."

"It could be an easy fix. Want me to take a look at it?"

"It's just a gas gauge. You wouldn't mind?" she asked.

"Not a bit. Help me save this stuff and I'll walk over with you to Joey's, and we can see what's going on with it."

"That would be great."

"But it will cost ya."

"Oh yeah? What will that be?'

"You have to take me on that trip."

Gabe and her on a motorcycle? Obviously, he would drive. Still, he would be right there. There was no personal space on a bike. Not if you wanted to ride comfortably. She said nothing at first.

"How about this?" Gabe conceded. "We'll work on it this afternoon. We can take a little spin. If it works, then we can a longer trip. You never know, I might drive like a maniac, and you may not want to hurtle down the highway with me."

She grinned. "I may like that."

He laughed. "Come on, help me carry this stuff up to the cabin and we'll get started."

She grabbed the tackle box and followed him to his cabin.

* * * *

HOURS LATER, AFTER a trip to the parts store, some wrench turning, and a lot of cursing, Gabriel was sitting on her motorcycle, revving the motor.

"I'm going to take it for a test spin," he said over the rumble. "I'll put some gas in it and come back. If you want, you can hop on then, and we'll take it for a drive."

As Grace watched him drive away, her anxiety intensified. She paced the driveway, waiting for him to come back. Could she be that close to him? What was she thinking? This was Gabe. Gabe who had been nothing but caring and gentle. She could do this. She would be damned if she'd let Brent ruin this for her like he'd ruined her singing career. She loved to ride. She would not let Brent win. Not this time.

She was still pacing when Gabe pulled up in the driveway. He smiled and held out his hand, "Come on, *cher.*"

Grace smiled, took a deep breath, and hopped on.

Sitting on the back of her own bike was weird at first. She couldn't remember the last time she had ridden as a passenger on her own bike. The experience of not being in control of the bike was unnerving.

Gabriel was a great rider, though, taking it nice and slow. Grace leaned in and out of the curves as they coasted along the highway that led through the town of Bon Chance. The beach lay on one side, the businesses and homes along the other. Freedom dead ahead. A sweet moment of peace as her head cleared and all worries and stresses drifted away. Grace closed her eyes as the wind rushed through her hair, lifting and blowing it behind her.

Gabe took them to the tip of the peninsula and pulled to a stop at a scenic outlook. "Wanna take a look around before we go back?"

"Sure." She slid off the bike and waited for him to do the same. Grace bent to take off her shoes and secured them in a saddlebag, as did Gabe.

The evening sun was setting, and the sky was an array of pastel blues, pinks, and yellows. A lone fishing boat was bobbing in the distance.

The sand was cool underneath her bare feet as she walked along the beach with Gabe. They were silent for a while, the only sound was the soft splash of the water as it hit the shore and receded back to the bay.

"Wanna sit?" Gabe asked as they approached a secluded spot that overlooked a fishing pier.

"Sure."

They sat down on the sand, close, but not too close. Grace leaned back and rested on her elbows and looked up at the sky. The sun was even lower on the horizon and the first stars now peeked out.

Gabe stretched out beside her. "Quiet, isn't it?"

"It is. I like it. So different from New Orleans. From the Quarter."

"Same here. Austin's pretty busy too."

"Do you miss Austin?"

"I do, actually. There's no place like it. Not even New Orleans. New Orleans is rough, gritty, old. Austin is trendy, new, eccentric. And I miss playing music."

Grace had to ask. "When do you go back?"

"October. We are playing the South by Southwest Festival."

October? It was September now.

Grace reached out and grabbed his hand. "Already? You're leaving so soon?"

Gabe's fingers interlaced with hers. "I am. I have to. You should come, Grace. Like I said, we're looking for a female vocalist. This could be our shot. Your shot."

Grace looked down at their entwined hands. For a moment, she thought of pulling back. She knew Gabe was interested in being more than friends. She also knew what a mess her head was right now.

"What if I can't?" Grace gave voice to the nagging fear that plagued her.

He squeezed her hand as he raised it to his lips. "You will, Grace. You will sing again. You have to find that faith in yourself again. The faith that I have. That all of us have in you."

Tears pooled in her eyes and she looked out at the waves. God, she hoped he was right.

Hand in hand, they finished watching the sunset in silence. When darkness finally fell, they returned to the motorcycle. As they rode, Grace wrapped her arms around Gabe's waist and rested her head on his back. She smiled the whole ride home.

• • • •

"SEEMS TO BE WORKING fine now," Gabe said as Grace hopped off the motorcycle.

"Thank you so much."

"So, how about that trip? I think I could use a little getaway myself."

"I would love to," Grace said, much to Gabe's surprise. "What do you have in mind?"

"We can think of something. How about we leave early and watch the sun rise as we ride, wherever we decide to go?"

"That sounds amazing," Grace said. "I'm looking forward to it already."

"Me too," he said. He stood there for a moment, unsure of what to do. He looked at her before giving her an awkward one-armed hug.

Grace wrapped her arms around him and hugged him for just a moment. "Thanks, Gabe."

"You're welcome," he said. When she let him go, he leaned down and lightly kissed her cheek. Progress. Gabe walked a few feet away then stopped and turned. He was smiling, and Grace couldn't help herself. She smiled back.

Chapter Sixteen

"First day teaching today?" Noah asked, handing her a mug of coffee then sitting down.

Grace took a sip of coffee before responding, "Yes."

If she could hear the indecision in her voice, she knew Noah's perceptive ass would pick up on it.

She had woken up before the alarm that morning, after a mostly sleepless night of tossing and turning. She had been so restless that even Furby had abandoned her and slept on a pillow on the floor.

The thought of standing in front of those kids filled her with panic. She had no clue what she was doing. More than once, she had considered calling Mr. Comeaux and telling him she had changed her mind. She was still debating as she sat on the houseboat with Noah. The cell phone laid on the table by her mug of coffee. All she would have to do is pick it up, dial, and say the words.

She was still staring at the phone when Noah began speaking. "When I retired from the Marines, I accepted a job with an oilfield company. The money was good, and the thought of fourteen days on and fourteen days off was appealing. As the day came closer for me to leave for work, I started having panic attacks every time I thought about being cooped up in those living quarters. I ended up turning it down."

He looked down at the mug he rolled back and forth in his palms. "After that, I took a job with a firm in New Orleans. Just routine security. That lasted all of a week, I think. New Orleans was too much for me. Too many people. Too much noise. So, I gave up on the job search. There's not a lot here to choose from. I had my retirement from the military. My houseboat and truck were paid for, so I didn't really need to work. But I found myself feeling adrift, just floating through life. And that didn't go over well with me, not after the structure of the military."

That was how she felt. Adrift. Like she was one big wave away from going under.

"One morning while on a run," Noah continued, "Glinda came out to meet me. She needed a few repairs, and with Gabriel in Austin, she wanted to know if I could help. I did a small roof repair. Next, it was a deck restore. I found myself enjoying the work. I loved working with my hands, and the solitude of working by myself was a bonus. I started renovating my boat. Finally, I had something I wanted to do. Somewhere to be. The panic attacks and nightmares came less frequently. For the first time since I came home, I felt moments of peace. Those moments became days, and later weeks. It took time, Grace. It didn't happen overnight. But I did find where I fit in."

He gestured to his empty mug of coffee. "I need a refill. You?"

Grace nodded. "I do. Just one. Then it looks like I need to get ready for work."

"Yes, you do." And with that, Noah went back into the boat for refills. Grace knew, that for now, talk time was over.

• • • •

AS GRACE WALKED THROUGH the double doors of the high school building, she pulled at her loose khaki pants. Always comfortable in jeans and concert t-shirts, she felt even more out of place than usual. When she was on stage she wore whatever fit her mood. Short black skirt and a shiny top. Or scarlet corset and leather pants when she was feeling badass.

She was not feeling badass today.

She felt like a fraud.

What the hell was she going to teach these kids?

Allison had given her some "first day" activities and an agenda. She would introduce herself. The questionnaire should keep them busy. It asked things like, *What do you want to learn? What's your favorite type of music? What are your hobbies?* They could do that.

She was off the first hour for planning. Which she loved. She hated mornings. She never felt human until around noon.

Coffee. I need coffee, she thought.

She nodded at the secretary and receptionist as she walked in but didn't speak. She headed straight for the teacher's lounge to fill her travel mug with coffee.

Grace had arrived early in order to avoid most people, and the lounge was still empty. She was filling up her mug when she heard the door open behind her. She turned to see who it was.

"Are you the new English teacher?" one of two girls said as they approached.

"Yes."

"Great!" the other said. "We are so excited. Are you going to teach us how to do research papers? We really need to learn how to do that. We didn't learn it last year. And most of us are going to college."

Research papers? Grace hadn't done a research paper since college years ago.

"Maybe so," Grace responded. It was a good noncommittal response.

"Great!" one exclaimed. They proceeded to introduce themselves, and Grace promptly forgot their names. Her mind was still stuck on "research paper."

They flashed Grace more grins and flittered out the door. Grace took a deep breath and sipped her coffee. This was going to be a long morning.

Grace sighed and walked to the room the principal had taken her to when she had interviewed. True to his word, the room was a clean slate. The tables gleamed, the walls were empty, and the room was almost sterile.

She put the flash drive in the computer by the teacher's desk. She pulled up the survey that Allison had emailed her and was waiting for it to print.

"Good morning!"

Grace turned as someone came into the room. It was an older woman with short grey hair. The woman smiled and looked way too energetic before noon.

"Morning," Grace said. There was nothing good about mornings. Grace looked at the woman, not returning the smile.

"I'm Ms. Edwards," the woman said, holding out her hand. "Mr. Comeaux said you would be here today. It's nice to meet you."

"I'm Grace."

"Grace, do you have any questions? Mr. Comeaux says this is your first teaching experience."

"It is."

"How exciting. You need some advice?"

No, not really, Grace thought, but said nothing.

The woman kept talking. "You need some procedures in place. The students need to know what your expectations are.

I have posters in my classroom. Sixteen classroom procedures. Everything from throwing away trash, to sharpening pencils, to handing in papers."

"What grade do you teach?" Grace asked.

"I teach physical science and biology, so I have everyone from ninth to twelfth graders."

"So, you're telling me that a senior needs to be told how to throw away trash?" Grace asked.

"Well, of course. If you don't tell them, they won't know how to do it right."

"There's a wrong way to throw away trash?"

"Well, of course."

Grace resisted the urge to laugh. She turned to grab the sheet from the printer. "It was so kind of you to come by this morning, but if you'll excuse me, I need to get copies made."

"Of course," the short woman said. "And if you need anything, please come see me. I'm in room twelve."

"Will do," Grace said. When hell froze over. Procedures. Grace shook her head as the woman walked out of the classroom.

It was going to be a long day.

· · · ·

GRACE WAS WAITING FOR the bell to ring and for the first group of students to come in. She straightened up the stack of papers on the desk for what must have been the tenth time. She only had to make it through today. One day at a time.

She looked at the piles of novels in the corner. She would make a list of those and discuss them with Allison, and maybe

Daniel. Maybe a novel and a movie would be a great way to ease into this job.

The bell rang. *Here we go.*

The students began filing in, all looking at her with curiosity. Their eyes seemed to be asking, *Who is this new person in this classroom?* She stood in front of the room as they all took their places at the u-shaped tables. Some teased each other quietly, elbowing each other.

The bell rang again, and they all looked at her expectantly.

Here goes nothing, Grace thought.

"Good morning," she said. "My name is Grace Delchamp, and it looks like I'll be your teacher for the rest of—well for now." "

"Do we call you Grace or Ms. Delchamp?" one student asked.

"Ms. Delchamp," Grace said.

"Is that Miss Delchamp or Mrs. Delchamp?" the same boy asked, and the few boys around him snickered.

Grace frowned and raised an eyebrow at the boy. "That would be Miss Delchamp," Grace said. "And you would be?"

"Jean Wayne." Jean, pronounced "John" in the French dialect.

"Jean Wayne?" Grace's eyebrow shot up again. "Is that right?"

"Yes, I'm rough and tough and don't take no crap off nobody."

The whole class snickered this time, and Grace bit back a smile herself.

"Well, Mr. Wayne," Grace said, "we'll just see how rough and tough you are, won't we?"

Grace grabbed the stack of papers on the corner of the desk. "This is your first assignment. And yes, I will read them. And yes, you will be graded. So I expect you to do it."

And with that, the class settled down and completed their work. Grace sighed, this was going to be a long week.

• • • •

GABE WAS SITTING ON the porch, strumming a guitar. He was singing softly along and thinking about Grace. He wondered how her first day was going. He had gotten a text earlier, a simple, *I'm here*. He figured he would get the whole story later.

"Hey, Gabe!" Glinda said as she approached, covered plate in hand. "You didn't come up for breakfast. You okay?"

"I'm okay. Did you need something?" Gabe looked down at his phone, worried he'd missed Glinda's text.

"No, it's all good for today. I woulda called if I needed you."

She sat down beside Gabe. "What's on your mind? Or should I ask, who is on your mind?"

He exhaled a deep breath and sat the guitar down beside him. "I wish Grace would tell me what's going on. She's talked to Ryder and Noah, but she won't talk to me."

"It may be easier for her to talk to them," Glinda said.

"Why?"

"They're safe to her. Both are like brothers. They don't want anything from her. You do. And I know you haven't done anything about it, although I don't know why, but she knows. And that can't be easy. What if she opens up to you? What happens when you leave?"

Gabe was silent for a while, considering that. Glinda was right. "What about the cook-off? She was doing better, even started to sing. Then Brent came in. I've never seen anything like it. She just ran out. She was terrified. It's bad, Grandma."

She patted him on the leg. "I know, Gabe. But she's tough. And so are you. I know this wasn't what you expected when you came home for her. That's life, Gabe. You don't always get what you expect. And wouldn't life be boring if you did?"

He nodded. "You right."

"It's all gonna work out, you'll see. You're just going to have to be patient. It's going to take some time, yeah. She needs to see you as steady, someone she can depend on. And that, my darling grandson, you are. Just keep being you, Gabe. The rest will fall into place."

She gave him a final pat on the knee and stood up. "Now, eat you some breakfast and let's go do some fishing. It's slow, and I need some sun. You're bringing the beer though."

Gabe laughed. "You got it, Grams. I'll come pick you up in half an hour."

"I'll be ready, *cher*! She who catches the most fish, wins!"

Gabe smiled and shook his head as she walked off toward the Redbird.

Chapter Seventeen

D*eepest are the wounds that that have no mark at all.*
Grace wrote the first line of lyrics in her journal and set the pen down. She looked out over the water, thinking of Gabe. She hadn't seen him all week, not since she'd started teaching, though they had text messaged back and forth. She hadn't even been to Snapper's. By the time she met with Noah for their morning "therapy" sessions, went to work, and took care of Furby, she ended up an exhausted lump in bed. Today was Friday, and she was looking forward to hanging out and having a drink at Snapper's with everyone later.

She looked out over the calm gulf that mirrored the morning's sunrise and yawned. She'd go to Snapper's if she squeezed in a nap after work.

She closed the journal.. She would see Gabe tonight. That thought brought a smile to her face.

"Smiling because it's Friday?" Noah asked, coming through the sliding glass doors, mugs in hand.

"I guess you could say that."

"You get some writing in?"

"I did."

"That's good," he said. "I'm working on something myself. Not writing though. Emily wants an outdoor kitchen with a patio area added to the house. A place for everyone to hang out for cookouts, shrimp and crawfish boils, you know. I'm working on drawing up some plans. We hope to have it mostly finished by Thanksgiving so we can have dinner there. Give Glinda a break."

"That's awesome. I bet she'll love it."

"Hope so. She's showed me about a hundred pictures from some app she has on her phone. Some pinning thing. It's going to have lots of seating, a fire pit, and a huge cypress table. I don't think I can get the table done by then, but I can get a lot of the rest done."

"I can't wait to see it."

"It feels good to be creating something. It gives me some focus. I've been thinking about opening a custom furniture business. I guess Emily's rubbing off on me."

She definitely was, Grace thought. He had changed so much in the last year since being with Emily.

"I just worry about working with the public. I still get antsy in crowds, still feel closed in sometimes. Em tells me to take it one day at a time. We'll see, I guess. I can always start small and go from there."

"That's true," Grace said, and thought how right that was. Small steps, one thing, one day at a time. That was what she was doing. It seemed to be working. For now.

Grace glanced back down at the journal lying on her lap. "You're right, Noah, it does feel good to create something." Grace had no idea if she'd ever be able to perform again, but for now, she could write. She opened the journal again, grabbed the pen, and wrote out some more lyrics, humming along as she wrote. Noah was silent, sipping his coffee, watching the sun finish rising.

· · · ·

GRACE CHECKED THE TIME on her watch as she walked into the school building after securing the bike by her classroom window. She had her helmet under one arm, black hair in a ponytail that swung behind her. Joey had needed the Jeep for a supply run for the weekend, and Grace wanted to make sure the bike was running well.

She had about five minutes before she had to meet Ms. Benoit in the home ec room for the homecoming sponsors meeting. How Grace had been selected to help with that she had no clue. Grace had only gone to her own homecoming dance because she and Gabe, and the rest of the band, had been asked to play. Grace was more inclined to sneak booze and cigarettes behind the bleachers with Carly than attend school functions. When Noah wasn't around to fuss, of course.

Grace stopped in her room to lock the helmet into the classroom cabinet. She then made her way down the hall to the home economics classroom.

"Holy shit," she whispered when she opened the door.

Someone had decorated the room in what Grace could only call "Grandma's Attic." White lace spilled over the room like a '70s style wedding dress had thrown up. It dripped down the walls and covered the windows. It was even draped on the student's tables. Antique tea kettles with floral designs sat on each of the four stoves the students used to cook. Posters adorned the wall with phrases like *Just Say NO* and other slogans that promoted abstinence and good behavior.

"You must be Grace Delchamp," said Mrs. Benoit as she stepped out from behind the desk. She was wearing an ankle length skirt, and even more lace adorned her shirt. Her brown hair was cut into a no-nonsense page boy, and the only adornment on her face was round black eyeglasses. No makeup. No lip gloss. Nothing.

"I am," Grace said. *And you must be repressed*, Grace thought. This woman probably hadn't been laid since that shirt was in style.

"We are just so excited to have a young person here on staff. Such a good influence for our young people." Ms. Benoit shook Grace's hand and saw the dangling charm bracelet.

"A charm bracelet! How cute! I wore one of these when I was young. Every charm meant something. May I?" She gestured to the bracelet, and Grace held up her wrist.

"Oh, angel wings!" she exclaimed, seeing the zombie show charm. "I had a pair of angel wings on my bracelet too!"

Grace choked on a laugh.

"Oh my!" Ms. Benoit said as she touched the next charm. Ryder had taken a Coors Light bottle cap and fashioned it into a charm for the bracelet.

"Is that a real beer bottle cap?" she asked.

"Yes, ma'am."

Ms. Benoit dropped her hand as if the bracelet was now poisoned.

"Well, we'd better get started," Ms. Benoit said, glancing at the old cuckoo clock that hung above the door. She took a deep breath, clasped her hands in front of her, and exhaled as if dealing with an unruly child.

"Ms. Delchamp. We have a rather conservative staff here."

No shit, Grace thought.

"And we like to encourage the best behavior in our students." She glanced at Grace's wrist. "We are, after all, role models for our youth."

Grace raised an eyebrow but said nothing. She wasn't taking the bracelet off. She let Ms. Benoit keep talking. Grace wondered what the woman would do if she knew Grace had a knife in her boot. Probably faint.

"Especially at extra-curricular activities, such as dances. We have very strict policies that we follow."

I bet you do.

"Even our music is hand-picked by myself and the other staff."

Probably music from the '50s. Grace wondered if their themes included sock hops and cowboys and Indians. Grace would bet that the woman owned a poodle skirt and saddle shoes.

Grace resisted the urge to roll her eyes. Seriously, how did she end up here?

"Your job is to make sure all information gets delivered to the students. And you will also handle the selection of the theme. The students vote on what they want. With our approval, of course."

Of course.

"Later, I will go over the rest of all this. I'm sure you have enough on your plate at the moment. Mr. Comeaux tells me this is your first year."

"It is."

"Well, welcome to Pointe Shade High," Ms. Benoit said. "I'll be checking in with you throughout the year."

"Lovely," Grace said with a tight smile and fake cheer. "I so can't wait."

It was Ms. Benoit's turn to shoot up an eyebrow, but she said nothing at Grace's sarcasm.

Grace returned to her room.

Thank God it's Friday. She grabbed her cell phone, leaned back in her chair and propped her feet on the desk. Her black boots thudded as they hit the desktop.

Man, this job blows, Grace said in a text to Gabe, twisting the charm bracelet.

Give it time, came his response.

The school bell rang and soon second hour was rolling in. Those rascals. She had already pegged this class as the trouble-makers. The ironic part was she didn't think she was much different than they were. She went to stand by the door as the kids came in, even more hyper than usual. It was Friday and game day. Grace just shook her head.

"Hey, Ms. Delchamp," one of the boys said as she started to close the door. "Lemme holla at dat girl who just pass by! She cute!"

"No," she said with a laugh as she shut the door. "Holla at her later."

After they all sat down after saying the pledge, Grace said, "It's Friday. That means vocabulary quiz."

"A quiz?" Jean Wayne asked. "Already?"

"Yes. Already."

"Now, surely, there's something we can do here. Some kind of deal we can make."

"Nope. No deals." She began passing out the quizzes. "Next Monday, we'll do our next vocabulary set and we'll start *The Great Gatsby*."

Several students groaned.

C'mon three o'clock, Grace thought.

• • • •

. AFTER DOING CARPENTRY work for Glinda all day, he couldn't wait to get in the shower and get cleaned off. Gabe dried off and wrapped the towel around his waist. He shrugged shoulders that were tight from swinging a hammer all day. He didn't know how Noah did it. Noah was used to it, Gabe thought. Gabe was not. He was not out of shape. He did work out but strumming a guitar and running on a treadmill was not the same as daily manual labor.

He had gotten a text from Bennet earlier. He was getting some gigs lined up for the holiday season to fill in between the tour dates. The holiday season was always busy with Christmas and New Year's parties.

But what about Grace?

Something was finally going on with the two of them. He was making progress, but it was slow. He could see her slowly coming out of dark place she had been. Maybe they could figure something out. Austin wasn't that far from Bon Chance. Maybe he could talk her into coming for a visit. If she liked it, maybe she could stay.

Gabe shook his head. That was a lot of maybes. Maybe he should just get dressed and head over to Snapper's. The future would just have to work itself out, as Glinda would say.

· · · ·

"I NEED A DRINK AND a shot of Patron," Grace told Carly as she sat down.

"That bad?"

"Oh my God," Grace said. "I don't know how I'm going to do another whole week of this next week."

"It should get easier," Carly said. "It's just something new."

"It's something, all right."

"Well, I'll get you that shot. It should help. Allison is coming tonight too. Y'all can talk about whatever it is schoolteachers talk about."

Grace laughed. "I am not a schoolteacher."

"You are for now, aren't you?"

Carly left to make the drinks and shots, and Grace leaned back in the barstool, resting her knees on the bar.

Carly returned with her drink and shot and had made a shot for herself as well. Carly never let anyone take shots alone.

They grabbed the small cups and tapped them against each other. "To Friday!" they said before downing the shots.

The Patron burned Grace's belly as it went down, and she fought a grimace. Patron tasted good, but it was potent.

Grace was still sitting there when Gabe showed up. Grace's heart sped up a little when she saw him walk through the door. He grinned when he saw her.

After exchanging handshakes with the regulars, he walked over to Grace, hugging her before he took a seat beside her.

Carly was quick to set a drink down in front of him. The bar had gotten busy for the Friday happy hour, so she didn't have time for casual chit chat, only a, "Hey how are you, and let me take your money."

"I see you survived your first week of work," Gabe said.

"Barely, I think. Man, I wanted something to keep me busy, and that's what I got. This homecoming thing is going to get crazy. Floats, dances, all that."

"You'll be fine."

"I'm glad you think so."

The side door opened and the DJ/karaoke guy started wheeling in his equipment. Behind him was Allison.

Grace smiled when she saw Allison walk in. "Thank God. I need some pointers. I don't know how much shop talk she'll want to do on a Friday night. I'm not extraordinarily excited about talking about school myself."

"So how did it go?" Allison asked after sitting down beside Grace.

"It was okay," Grace said. She gave Gabe and Allison a review of the week. She told them about the procedure Nazi, the unruly second hour, and the home ec teacher.

"I told you they were conservative," Allison said, laughing.

"I didn't think they would be that bad! It is like something out of that movie *Footloose*. Oooh, speaking of which, we should play some of that on the jukebox tonight."

"Definitely," Allison agreed. "There's the preacher's daughter and everything. She's already tweeted about me and everything from what the kids have told me."

"Seriously?" Gabe asked.

"Yeah. I made a remark sometime during the week about gay people after the subject of my predecessor came up. Said I didn't care what people did. Girl posted that teachers should not be putting such ideas in young people's heads."

Grace shook her head. "No wonder the dude went nuts. I may be running around in the park naked myself by the end of the year."

"You'll be fine," Gabe said. "If you can handle all those Bourbon Street drunks, you can handle this."

"I hope so. Let's talk about something else for a little while. How about we play the jukebox too? I'm ready to relax."

"Sounds great," Gabe said, reaching for his wallet for some cash. "I'll do first round. You just sit and enjoy."

"He's cute," Allison said as he walked away.

"Yes, he is," Grace agreed.

"And the way he looks at you..."

"What do you mean?"

"Girl? You can't see it?"

"Gabe?"

"Gabe."

Grace turned in her stool to look at him. She thought of the looks and glances, the touches. Gabe? How long had he been interested in her and she not see it? She turned back around in her stool and sipped her drink. "He is sweet. And cute."

Allison laughed. "Not many cute *and* available guys come into Snapper's. I'm partial to Noah's friend, Douglas, myself."

Grace grinned. "You should go for him."

"Oh, I'm going to. I think I might start by inviting him to talk to my students one day."

"There ya go," Grace said. "I can put a little bug in Noah's ear as well."

"Nah, not yet. Let's see how it goes after the visit."

Grace lifted her glass in a salute. "Let's cheers to that."

"To new beginnings," Allison said.

"To new beginnings," Grace agreed.

"You guys are toasting without me?" Carly exclaimed. "Hang on!"

Carly returned with a beer. "What are we toasting to?"

"New beginnings," Allison said.

"Hell yeah!"

The girls lifted their drinks in the air and clinked them together.

"To new beginnings!" they said in unison.

• • • •

FINISHED AT THE JUKEBOX, Gabe turned back to the bar. He froze when he saw Grace smile as she toasted with the girls.

It was a genuine smile, one of the few he'd seen lately. His stomach flip-flopped seeing that old familiar light in her eyes. She was coming back from wherever dark place she had been. He was smiling too as he rejoined them at the bar.

"What did you play?" Grace asked as he sat down.

"You'll see," he replied. "A little bit of this, a little bit of that." He had played songs he had heard her play on the jukebox before and a few of his own favorites. Nothing too serious. He wanted to be sure that she had a good time. He just wanted to see that smile she was wearing stay right where it was.

"How was your day?" she asked him.

He shrugged sore shoulders. "Glinda kept me busy today. I did several repairs. Now that the season is dying down there are more vacant cabins to do general maintenance on."

"I'm sure she loves having you here."

"She does." He patted his stomach. "I've been well fed. If I keep this up, I'm going to have to start working out with all this manual labor."

"Oh, let me see." Grinning, Grace leaned over and put her hand on his stomach. His stomach tensed under her soft touch. Her hand stilled, and her eyes shot up to meet his.

Her smiled slipped then, her eyes filling with something that wasn't humor. She bit her bottom lip, and Gabe had to resist bending down and placing his lips on hers.

"Hey, guys! You singing tonight?"

Gabe muttered a quiet curse as the karaoke guy placed a huge binder between Grace and him, along with small strips of paper and pencils.

Grace inhaled a breath like she'd been punched in the stomach. She took a long drink, then replied, "No. I won't be singing tonight."

"Maybe later," Gabe said to the DJ, and was relieved when he moved on to the next group.

He took a long sip of his own drink.

Damn, damn, damn.

So much for progress.

Chapter Eighteen

Grace took *The Great Gatsby*, along with her writing journal, and walked down the beach. It was Sunday and she wanted to read a little of the book before she started with the students. Allison had sent her some plans, and with a little reading today, Grace felt pretty comfortable with the next week.

She took a moment to stretch and enjoy the view. The sun was beginning to set, and the pastels were reflected on the water. She had just leaned back and opened the book when a shadow fell across her. It was Gabe. He dropped down on the sand beside her.

"Whatcha reading?" he asked.

"This book," she said, showing him the cover.

"*The Great Gatsby*, huh? I think I remember reading that in high school," he said.

"We read this?" she asked.

"Yes, in junior English. You don't remember because you slept. Then cheated off me on the tests."

"I did?" she asked.

"Yes, you did," he said. "Then they made us watch some crappy old movie with Robert Redford."

"Oh, I remember that," she said. "Sorta. It's amazing I made it through college."

Gabe grinned. "I know, right?"

"Actually, I didn't mind college. I didn't feel so different there. More people like me. I think that's why I like my second hour so much. They remind me of myself when I was that age.

The whole class actually. They're a bunch of rebels who speak their minds."

"You? A rebel? No..." His eyes widened in pretend shock.

She slapped him on the arm with the book. "Shut up. What did you bring to drink? I could definitely use a drink now."

He poured a Southern and Seven from his ice chest and handed it to her.

"It's not so bad though," she said finally.

"What isn't?" he asked.

"The job. I've had worse. And the kids are fun."

"That's what matters, isn't it?"

"I guess so."

He leaned down on the sand beside her, resting on his elbows. "I talked to Bennet on Friday. He's lining up some more gigs. You should come visit. You have those breaks at school. You could sit in with us."

"Already?" The thought of him not being there made her uneasy. She had come to enjoy his gentle presence. She looked at him, and he was frowning at her.

"I need to get back to Austin. To the band. To my job."

Grace nodded. She understood. She didn't like it though. She took another drink.

"Not too soon though.".

"And Maybe I'll take a trip out to Austin for the holidays"

"Come to Austin. See how you like it You may want to stay."

Leave Bon Chance again? She had just started to regain her footing. Thinking about leaving again made her heart race and palms sweat. She couldn't move. She was safe here.

"I don't know."

Gabe reached out and grabbed her hand, threading her fingers in his. "Grace, you don't have to make any decisions now. If you don't come, you don't. But I will tell you this. If you don't come to Austin, I will come back here. For you."

Grace's eyes widened.

"I came back here for you. Don't look at me like you're shocked. I was crazy about you in high school, and I never said anything. I let you walk away, run away to New Orleans. I've always regretted it too. I'm not doing that again. I'm not pressuring you though. We aren't going to do anything you aren't ready to do."

He let go of her hand to reach out and lift her chin up. He leaned down and placed a soft, gentle kiss on her lips.

"I know something bad has happened to you. I hope one day you'll trust me enough to tell me. And I'm willing to be patient. I've waited this long. What's a little longer?"

Tears pricked Grace's eyes, and she looked away from him back to the water.

"It was Brent. We had been arguing for a while. He kept coming on to me and I turned him down. He got tired of waiting, I guess."

She stopped to wipe a tear away, and Gabe's hand reached for hers.

"He put something in my drink one night. And the next morning, I woke up with him naked in my bed. Not remembering anything. I still don't. I think that might be the worst. I know we had sex and I can't remember anything." She stopped talking for a few moments.

"I don't know if I can do this." Her voice was soft and hoarse when she continued.

Gabe reached out and wrapped an arm around her shoulders, and she leaned into him.

Gabe's voice was ragged when he responded, "Not I, Grace. We. We can do this. And we will. Together."

Grace's eyes welled up and spilled over with tears, and Gabe's hold on her tightened.

"Gabe? I will come visit. I can't make any promises to stay. But I can't sing. Until I can, I can't leave here."

"That's enough for me."

She sat there wrapped in his arms as the sun set, the moon rose, and the stars popped out in the night sky. When she finally shivered from the chill, he helped her to her feet and walked her home.

"Night, Grace," he said before placing a kiss on her lips, then her forehead before walking home.

Chapter Nineteen

Grace snapped the notebook shut and turned to Noah. "Why should I write if I'm not going to ever be able to perform? Why can't I sing anymore without wanting to throw up?"

"It's all in your head, Grace."

"What do you mean?"

"You have to figure out the 'why' on your own. I don't know what it is, but it's something you're going to have to face. When you finally confront it, you'll find your voice again. And you will be better. You'll see."

"You think so?" Grace stared out at the sunrise while she waited for Noah's answer.

"I know so." Noah reached over and opened the drawer on the small table between the two chairs. He pulled out a pack of cigarettes. Grace's eyes widened.

"We're going to do some talking this morning. Want one?" He held one out to her.

"What about Emily? What will she think about you smoking?"

"It's a cigarette, Grace. I picked it up in Iraq. It's not something I do often, just every now and then. I smoke on certain anniversaries. The days I lost friends. Benjamin. She understands."

He was still holding the cigarette out. Grace took it. He lit it for her. She felt the burn as she inhaled.

"It's one of those anniversaries for me today," Noah said. "I lost a friend, a brother, three years ago today. He was one of the kids in my command. I say kid, he wasn't much younger than I was at the time. I was there. I saw it. Saw the explosion. Felt the heat on my face as the vehicle burned."

He was quiet for a moment, just drinking his coffee and taking the occasional drag from the cigarette.

"I went home with him. With his body. All the way to the funeral home. Saw his family come in after we brought him home. I don't think I'll ever forget their faces. The sister who sat sobbing in one of the back pews of the funeral home. I didn't think I'd ever forget my guilt. If I had done this, or changed that, then I wouldn't be there at that moment. And he'd still be alive. They wouldn't be grieving, and neither would I."

He took another drag off the cigarette. Grace watched the smoke drift off into the pre-dawn light. She still said nothing.

"I had nightmares about it for so long. Saw him. The explosion. I could smell the flames, they were so real. Saw the family. Saw it over and over. Until it almost made me crazy. Finally, I realized I had to let it go. I had done everything I could at the time. Life sucks sometimes. It just does. We have to deal with the hand we're given."

Grace still said nothing, unsure of what to say. She just continued to drink coffee and take an occasional puff off the cigarette. Noah had never spoken this much to her about anything, much less about what he had been through.

He took another long drag off the cigarette. "I had to face my demons, Grace. I had to figure out what I needed to do to let them go and make peace. So one night, I sat here on this beach. I made a fire and drank and watched the fire. And just sat there until all my ghosts were gone for the moment. It was a purge."

He stubbed the cigarette out. "You're going to have to purge your demons. How you do that is up to you. I can't tell you how. And I can't say your life will be easy after that. Mine isn't. But you won't find peace or your voice until you do. I believe eventually you will. You have all of us here to help you. And you're strong, Grace. You've just lost your faith in yourself."

He reached into the drawer again and pulled out a small round charm. He held it out to Grace. It was a small globe with and eagle and an anchor. The Marine Corps symbol.

"I took this and made you a charm. Whenever you feel like you need a little faith in yourself, remember Semper Fi. *Always faithful.*"

Grace took a final drag off the cigarette and stubbed it out.

"I don't know what to say," she said. "I can't imagine what you've been through. But thank you. For everything."

"You're welcome. I don't talk about it much," he said. "Maybe this will help you."

After that they fell into the comfortable silence that was now their morning habit. A little bit of conversation, then a lot of silence. Grace reopened the journal, hoping the words would continue to flow. She would sing again, and she would sing the words she had written.

• • • •

GRACE NURSED A CUP of coffee and looked at the clock on the classroom wall. The clock was the only adornment on the beige walls. She still had not done anything to make the room her own.

She had about five minutes before her first class came in. She needed the extra caffeine, as that class was something else. She was glad she was off first hour, then started with them and got them out of the way. They had been more unruly than usual. Homecoming was fast approaching. The big parade float competition had all the classes talking trash to each other. Grace wanted to see her kids win. They were the constant underdogs, the smallest class, the misfits, but they had the biggest heart. Grace was always a sucker for the underdog.

They had been working tirelessly after school to get the float ready. Grace had helped as much as she could, but really the sponsors weren't supposed to help. They had chosen an '80s theme, which she loved. She had heard most of the other classes had chosen fishing and hunting themes. Or themes based on popular shows. She was glad that her class had chosen something different.

The bell rang, and soon the students began taking their seats.

"Ms. Delchamp, are you staying after school again today so we can work on our float?" one student asked as he walked in.

"Yes. I have a faculty meeting, but I'll be there when we finish." Grace wanted to see them win so badly that she didn't even mind staying an extra hour or two after work.

"Awesome."

"It doesn't matter," Jean Wayne said. "We're going to win anyway."

Jean Wayne was one of the few seniors in English III. He always had to stir the pot and put his two cents in.

Grace rolled her eyes before adding, "We'll see about that, won't we?"

"It's how it is. We're seniors, and seniors always win. It's tradition."

"So, what you're saying is the seniors could take a float out with absolutely nothing on it but people, and you guys would still win?"

"That's exactly what I'm saying."

"That's stupid," Grace said. "You guys should do something to change that."

"That's the way it is."

"Some things need to change." She smiled. "You guys are the rebels."

"We are. But still, you can't fight tradition," another student spoke up.

Grace shook her head. This was exactly why she had not been a big participant in high school functions. She did what she had to do to get by and played gigs on the weekend. The announcements ended the conversation.

"So, Ms. Delchamp," John Wayne said when the announcements were over, "I read on Twitter that you used to be a lead singer for a band in New Orleans on Bourbon Street!"

"Is that right?" Grace asked.

"That's what I heard."

"Ah, the lovely Twitter Queens," Grace said, resisting the urge to roll her eyes again. "I'm not going to lie. Yes, my background is music, and yes, I sing and play bass. And yes, I did play on Bourbon Street."

"That's badass!" another student exclaimed. "You should sing for us sometime. You could sing on our float for the homecoming parade! It would be epic! Something Pointe Shade has never seen!"

Grace's stomach tightened. If she hadn't lost her voice, she would volunteer to sing on the float. Wouldn't that turn some heads? She could do a medley. Some Joan Jett, Pat Benatar, Lita Ford. A little song from *Footloose*. That would be hilarious.

"Watch your mouth," Grace said. "And no. I'm out of the band business for now. Speaking of bands, let's talk big bands and the nineteen twenties. If you'll open your Gatsby books, we'll get started. We will be reading about bands and booze today."

"Ms. Delchamp," a student said, "are you sure we should be reading this? My grandma said it's putting ideas in our heads about drinking and promiscuity."

"These ideas were in the twenties. It's history. I don't see the problem," Grace said. "Now let's get started."

• • • •

"AND THAT'S IT FOR TODAY, guys and girls," Grace told the last class after they had finished their reading for the day. Her last class was the girly girls. Complete opposites from Grace, except for their drive. They finished their work early daily. She was convinced if she gave them a lesson plan and book, they could teach themselves.

As always when they were finished, the talk turned to the most important event for high school students that time of year. Homecoming. Who was going to be on the court this year? Who was going to be queen and ride in that convertible wearing the white dress and crown?

Again, they were complete opposites from Grace, who would rather die than be put in heels and a flouncy dress. Grace shook her head and grabbed her phone. She leaned back in her chair and put her booted feet up on the desk.

Grace: They're talking about homecoming again.
Gabe: Lol. I can see you rolling your eyes.
Grace: Yes.

One of the girls said, "I heard that Precious bought the vote, if you know what I mean."

"That doesn't surprise me," said another, with a raise of one perfectly contoured eyebrow.

Grace shook her head again. Precious Mouton was the local preacher's daughter. She fit the stereotype well. She posted on social media regularly about God, religion, and overall general damnation, but had the offline reputation of a Bourbon Street hooker. Grace had heard that Precious had mentioned her on Twitter on more than one occasion. She had also heard that Ms. Benoit had made a few comments about her as well about being a proper role model and rebellious tendencies. Grace didn't give a damn about any of it.

All homecoming talk ended as the final bell rang. After the students filed out, Grace grabbed her backpack and keys. It was time to go to the school library for the faculty meeting. She took her normal spot in the back of the room. Being a new teacher, she hadn't become a part of a group yet. As most of the faculty had been here for years, there was a definite grouping of people. The coaches sat at one table, reading the paper and talking sports. There was another group of people at another table who had grown up in the town. Grace's table in the back consisted of the odds and ends, the people who hadn't graduated from the school or been there long enough to be accepted as one of their own. The only thing new was the presentation projected on the board behind the principal that read *Homecoming*.

Thank goodness it was Thursday and the week was almost over, she thought. She just had to make it one more day.

Grace grabbed her journal and earbuds out of the backpack, deciding to doodle and go over lyrics she had written and to brainstorm other lines while she waited for the meeting to begin. She put one bud in so she could hear what was going on, and she continued to scribble in the notebook.

Mr. Comeaux walked in and took his normal faculty meeting place at the front of the room, and the quiet chit chat in the room ceased.

"Good afternoon," he said. He continued with a few general announcements about homecoming scheduling and other school business. "Now, Ms. Benoit would like to make a presentation."

She took the place in the front of the room. "Thank you Mr. Comeaux. Now, as you all know the students are gearing up for homecoming."

She pointed the remote to start the slideshow. The first slide was a picture of Leonardo DiCaprio playing Jay Gatsby in *The Great Gatsby* movie holding a glass of champagne in a toast. Grace had seen the pic all over social media. What she'd never seen before, however, was the big red circle with a slash on it. Like a no smoking sign, but this symbolized no fun.

Ms. Benoit looked at Grace. "As I said, homecoming is coming up, and we all know what that means for our young adults. It is our job to instruct them and guide them to proper behavior."

All eyes in the room turned to look at Grace as well. Grace shrugged. She leaned back in the chair. Still looking Ms. Benoit in the eye, she raised her water bottle in a toast. She smiled and shook her head.

It's going to be one long year, Grace thought again.

Chapter Twenty

The spotlight was on Grace, the heat and the light surrounded her in a warm glow. Her head lowered, she waited for her cue as the music began playing.

It was time. She opened her mouth to sing but no words would come out. Her eyes widened as she looked out at the expectant crowd. She tried again. Still nothing. Her heart pounded and pulse raced as she tried in vain to make some kind of sound.

Nothing.

"I told you, you will never sing again," Brent said from behind her.

Grace broke out in a cold sweat at the sound of his voice. He moved closer. Grace could feel his body pressed against her back.

Grace turned, his presence so close it made her want to run out of the nearest door, but she didn't. She looked him in the eye.

"Yes, Brent. I will sing again, I promise you that. I promise me that." She shoved the microphone at him and walked away, leaving him alone on the stage in silence.

· · · ·

GRACE WALKED INTO SNAPPER'S after work. Ryder had sent a text earlier to meet him to celebrate. He hadn't said what the celebration was for, but apparently it was good news because Noah was there, along with Glinda and Daniel. Gabe was there too. She returned his smile before sitting down beside him, despite the funky mood she found herself in that night.

"How was your day?" he asked.

"I survived and so did the others," she said. Fridays were always interesting, especially with pep rallies and class rivalry. The faculty meeting with Ms. Benoit, her nightmare, and the kids asking that morning again to sing had left her nerves fragile and raw.

"That doesn't sound good," Gabe said.

She shook her head. "I just need a couple of drinks and to forget about it for a while." She turned to Ryder. "What's this big news?" she asked him.

He smiled. "You'll see."

Allison joined them then, Douglas behind her. Carly greeted them, then went to play DJ on the jukebox. A few of the guys grouped around the pool table, and the girls took spots by the bar.

"So, how's the writing coming along?" Grace asked Carly when she came back.

"It's going. I'm about to send out my weekend test text."

"Your what?" Allison asked.

"My test text," Carly said. "I started it two years ago when I was writing *All I Want for Christmas is a Real Good Man*. When I haven't been on a date in a while, I send out a general message to all the single men in my phone and see who responds. If I'm not dating, I can't write a dating book!"

Grace shook her head. "And then?"

"Then I go from there," Carly said. "I journal about it. And hopefully, a date."

Carly just didn't get it, Grace thought.

Carly looked at Allison. "I saw you come up with Douglas. Did you guys come together?"

"No, we just happened to drive up at the same time."

"He's single, you know," Carly said with a wink. Then looked at Grace. "And so is Gabe."

"Ryder is single too," Grace said to Allison. "So is Joey."

Grace smiled at Carly and her face clouded over. Good, Grace thought. Maybe it was time matchmaker Carly got a dose of her own medicine.

"I think it's time for that text," Carly said, frowning.

Emily arrived next. After a brief stop by Noah to give him a quick hello, she joined the girls.

"How's it going?" Carly asked.

"Business is good. I brought some food I made for client samples today. I'll get the guys to unload it in a little bit."

"Food? Did I hear food?" Ryder sat on Emily's lap and shoved his black cowboy hat on her head.

"So, Ms. Emily, any potato salad on the menu today?"

Emily smiled and smacked him on the arm. "It's samples for my Thanksgiving menu. Potato salad has nothing to do with Thanksgiving."

"It does if it involves getting naked." Ryder flashed her a grin. "I'm always thankful when I'm around a naked woman."

Emily shook her head and pushed him off her lap. "Go on, there are *single* women around."

"But they aren't cooking for me."

Emily handed him the hat back and stood up. "I'm going to get the guys to unload the van."

Ryder moved down to Allison. "What about you? Wanna get naked and throw potato salad?"

Allison shook her head and laughed. "I'm good."

"I bet you are. So am I." He grinned and raised one dark eyebrow.

She socked him in the arm too, saying, "That's not what I meant."

He donned his hat again and nodded to the ladies. "Anyone else?"

They all shook their heads.

He sighed. "You don't know what you're missing."

He tipped his hat and left to help the guys unload Emily's van. When everything was brought in, he came back to Grace.

"Come see," he said. "I'm going to tell you my news first."

He led her to a spot in the corner, away from the crowd and the noise. He put his hand on her arm. "I got a job offer today. It's a good opportunity. And a raise."

"That's great!" Grace exclaimed and hugged him.

"But," he said, and Grace's stomach flip-flopped.

"But?"

"I have to go to Houston. For weeks at a time."

Grace stopped breathing for a moment, the pain in her chest so overwhelming. "You're leaving."

"I have to. I can't pass it up. Who knows when another job offer will come up?"

Grace sucked in a breath, knowing he was right. She could do this. She could handle him being gone. It was just Houston.

"I'm happy for you," she said, and hugged him again. "It's just Houston."

He lifted her chin up to look at him. "Grace, I'll still be here for you, you know that."

She felt the sting of tears but blinked them away. "I know." She laid her head on his chest for a moment. "I'm still going to miss you though," she said when she lifted her head.

"I know," he said, his cheeky smile back in place.

She punched him in the chest. "Ass. I'm going back over there with the others."

A slow '80s power ballad started playing on the jukebox. Perfect for slow dancing. Carly's doing of course. Grace wondered who she would try to pair up for this one.

"Wanna dance?" Gabe asked as she returned to her seat.

She nodded. "Sure."

They joined Emily, Noah, Joey, Carly, and, surprisingly, Allison and Kevin on the small dance floor.

She moved along to the slow beat, enjoying the comfort of Gabe's embrace. As he felt her relax, he moved closer. Grace stiffened in reflex and missed a step. His disappointed sigh only served to intensify her general bad mood. Why couldn't she just enjoy this dance? Why did she have to add "can't dance with Gabe" to the growing list of things she couldn't do anymore. Sing, sleep, function as a normal woman and enjoy an attractive guy's embrace.

The now awkward and stiff dance finally ended and Grace returned to her seat. She ordered a shot and another drink. She turned away from the group to face the bar, sipping her drink. The bartender returned with the shot, and she gulped it down, feeling the burn all the way down. She slammed the glass down on the bar.

"You okay?" Gabe asked as he resumed his seat beside her.

"I am going to sing tonight, damnit," she said.

His eyebrows shot up in surprise. "Okay. What are you going to sing?"

"I don't know yet. Where are those books?"

"I'll get you one."

Grace ordered another shot as he disappeared to retrieve a karaoke book for her. He returned and sat the big binder in front of her.

"Want me to sing with you?"

She shook her head. "No. I need to do this. On my own."

He nodded and reached out to run his hand up her arm. "You got this, Grace."

She flipped through the pages, looking for a song. Looking for something that didn't bring up any memories or feelings. She settled on an old Stevie Nicks tune. She wrote it down and dropped it off at the karaoke table.

She resumed her seat and waited for the song playing to finish. While she waited, she gave herself a mental pep talk. She could do this. All she had to do was open her mouth and let the words come out. It wasn't hard. She had done it hundreds of times.

The final notes of the song faded out, and the DJ was announcing her name.

She took a deep breath and walked with her head high to the stage.

She took the mic in hand, enjoying the familiar feel of the metal. She kept her gaze on the TV screen, waiting for her cue to sing. The white letters of the song title and artist flashed on the blue screen and Grace took a deep breath. *Breathe in, breathe out*, she told herself.

The title screen disappeared, and the lyrics appeared on the screen.

Grace opened her mouth to sing the first few words. Nothing would come out. Horrified, she looked out at the crowd. Her heartbeat faster, as her mind locked up. The concern on her friends' faces only made it worse. She tossed the mic to the DJ.

Enraged, Grace turned and ran out the side door of the bar, took a few steps, and stopped. She looked up at the sky, the cold air cutting through her lungs as she took in deep breaths. The pain of the cold actually felt better than the pain she felt inside.

She couldn't sing. She couldn't do this. Ryder and Gabe were leaving. Gabe, who could sing, and she could not.

The soft sound of footsteps across the rocky parking lot told her someone had followed her outside. She knew who. Gabe and Ryder.

She refused to turn around to greet them.

She stiffened when she felt a hand on her shoulder but still refused to turn.

"Grace." It was Gabe. She didn't respond.

When she didn't answer, he moved to stand in front of her. He said again, "Grace."

She crossed her arms over her chest. She looked to the side, refusing to look him in the eye.

He reached out to touch her cheek, and her hand flashed up, grabbing it. "Don't touch me. Why do you even want to? Why are you even trying? Can't you see there's something wrong with me? I'm broken."

She looked him in the eye then, knowing all her anger and pain showed even in the dim moonlight. She smelled cigarette smoke on the light breeze and knew that Ryder was there as well. He just hadn't spoken up yet.

"Go away," she said to both of them. "You're both leaving anyway. You both get to go on with your lives and I'm stuck. Stuck here in this place I can't get out of."

Gabe took a step back, saying nothing. She felt a slight pang of guilt as his head dropped, knowing she had hurt him.

"Is that what this is about?" Ryder said finally.

She spun around, facing him. "Does it matter?"

He shook his head and flung his cigarette down, grounding it out with his boot. "At this point it doesn't, does it? You're going to do what you're going to do, and there's not a damn thing either of us," he nodded at Gabriel, "can do about it. But you can't expect us to quit living our lives because you can't get on with your own."

"Ryder," Gabriel started.

"Gabe," Ryder said. "This has gone on long enough. She needs to put on her big girl panties and deal."

"And how am I supposed to do that?" Grace sneered at him.

"Deal with it."

Grace took a step back, the itch to hit him strong.

Ryder raised an eyebrow, warning her, "Don't do it."

Grace felt tears sting and threaten to spill out. She looked away.

"Cry, Grace. Let it go," Ryder said.

Grace's eyes went wide. She looked everywhere but at Ryder. When she did look up at him, she saw the despair in his brown eyes. She wanted desperately to throw herself into his arms like she had done many times in the past when hurt.

"Fuck you," she said, and turned and walked away.

• • • •

HE AND RYDER WATCHED her disappear back down the beach. Ryder pulled a cigarette out of the pack and lit it. Gabe went to stand beside him. They stood there silently.

Gabe heard more footsteps behind them but didn't turn. Soon, a drink was being pressed into his hand. He looked to see Carly's troubled gaze also looking down the horizon to where Grace had disappeared. Noah and Joey had also come outside.

"I'm going after her," Gabe said.

"No," Ryder said on an exhale of smoke.

Gabe looked over to Noah, whose face was blank. "She needs to do this on her own, she needs to find that faith in herself. She's not going to move on, or sing," he looked at Gabe on that, "until she does."

Carly reached out and put her hands on his arms. "I have to get back in guys. It's busy. Keep an eye on our girl, okay?"

Gabe smiled, putting his hand on Carly's. "Of course."

Carly went back into the bar. Ryder made no move to leave, so Gabe didn't either. He stood beside Ryder, sipping his drink occasionally, not speaking. All of them focused on the house down the beach.

Gabe's drink was about halfway finished when he saw movement on the beach. It was Grace.

They moved closer and watched as she carried a trash bag to the beach. She pulled the bag open and black sheets spilled out onto the beach. He watched as she kicked the sheets into a pile. After that, she took a can of charcoal lighter fluid and poured it onto the sheets. She lit a match, watched the flame for a second, then pitched it onto the pile of sheets she had assembled. In a flash of light, the sheets went up in flames. Gabe could hear the flames flicker and spark from where he stood.

Grace took out a bottle of champagne and uncorked it, throwing the cork on the flames as well and tilting the bottle to her lips. She drank from the bottle until it was gone. Then, angry again, tossed the bottle on the fire as well.

She looked up again, and in the light of the fire, Gabe could see the tears flowing down her face. She dropped down on the sand to her knees. Her dark hair was a shroud around her. Gabe took a step toward her. Hands on either side of him stopped him.

A bottle of whisky appeared on his left.

"Semper Fi," Noah whispered, staring out at the water. "Semper Fi, Grace."

Gabe took a swig of the liquor, feeling the burn all the way down. He handed the bottle to Ryder.

Chapter Twenty-One

When Grace woke up, she was still on the beach. On the cold, morning breeze, she caught the scents of smoke—cigarette and the remnants of the fire she burned the night before. Ryder was there, somewhere in the shadows. She didn't even look around for him. Gabe probably was there too. She refused to acknowledge their presence, not a nod or a glance.

She looked at the dark spot of ashes. Tears pricked again. She had never felt so alone. So empty.

Gabe was leaving. So was Ryder. She'd never really been alone before, now she was, and was stuck. She looked out at the horizon. A new day. What would this day bring?

When there was no lingering smell of smoke, she knew Ryder was gone.

She grabbed the empty champagne bottle, still warm from the fire. She walked to the surf and filled it with the cool water of the gulf. She walked over to the ashes and poured the water on the remains. Watched the black and gray remnants wash away.

Only when she thought they were both gone did she let the tears fall again.

Grace felt a hand on her shoulder, and she looked up to see Gabe. He held a jacket that he draped across her shoulders. It was warm and smelled like him. He reached down and wiped the wet streaks from her face, then held out his hand to help her up, and she took it.

"Where's Ryder?"

"He went home."

"You guys were out here all night?"

He nodded. "Where else would we be? Where would I be?"

"Gabe," she started. He stopped her by placing a finger to her lips.

"You don't have to say anything or explain. You're coming to my house. I'm going to brew some coffee. You can shower if you want. And I have a surprise for you after that."

"A surprise?"

"Yes. Ryder, myself, Noah, Joey, and Carly cooked up something for you." He smiled. "We didn't have much else to do since none of us were going anywhere. Come on," he tugged her hand, "let's get started with today. Today is all about you, Grace."

She nodded and let him lead her to his cabin.

When they got there, Gabe set about making coffee. "Carly brought you a change of clothes and other things. They're in a bag on my bed. By the time you finish, coffee and breakfast will be ready."

Her stomach growled at the thought of food and coffee. She was starving.

He nodded to the bedroom. "Go on.'

She went in the bedroom and closed the door. There was a travel bag on his bed, just like he said. She opened it and was surprised to see more than one change of clothes and toiletries. What was going on?

She opened the door. "Gabe? What's all this in this bag?"

"Relax, Grace. I promise you can trust me."

He was right, she could trust him. She took the black t-shirt, jeans, and the toiletries and went to shower the sand, grit, and memories of the night before away.

Later, she walked into the living room, barefoot, and toweling off her hair. She took a seat at the bar. Nervous, she drummed her fingers against the tile.

Gabe sat a cup of coffee in front of her. He pushed a plate of biscuits, toast, and other breakfast goodies in front of her. "Eat something. You'll feel better."

"Gabe, what are we doing today? I saw the bag."

"We are going to Lafayette today. You said you wanted to go to Festival Acadiens one day, and it's this weekend. We're getting out of town."

Her heart raced at the thought of leaving town. It was Lafayette, though. Not New Orleans, not someplace that would bring on memories.

"It's time to step out again, Grace," he said.

She looked down, and when she did, she saw the Semper Fi charm on her bracelet. *Always faithful*, she thought. She raised her head and looked Gabe in the eye. She nodded. It was time to have a little faith, in herself and in Gabe.

"Let's do this," she said.

Gabe winked at her over the rim of his coffee cup. "Let me get my own shower and get ready, and we'll hit the road, *cher*."

• • • •

THE SOUNDS OF THE FIDDLE and accordion rang out from the multiple stages set up in the Lafayette park, and the spicy scents of Cajun cooking filled the air. Festival Acadiens was underway. Locals had set up colorful tents and canopies around the perimeter of the park, most sporting the red pepper Ragin' Cajun mascot. They were an oasis to rest and cool off after spending hours of dancing and drinking in the hot October sun. Kids tossed footballs back and forth. Couples lay on blankets spread out on the grass.

Gabe snagged a music schedule, and they found a place away from the crowd to look it over. Grace pointed out bands she wanted to see, and they put together a schedule for the day.

"Geno Delafosse plays in half an hour. You want to go ahead and go to that stage? I know he draws a crowd," Gabe said.

"Sure," she agreed.

As they approached the stage, Grace saw that Gabe had been right, there was already a small crowd beginning to gather. Some had already begun to dance to the music playing from the loudspeakers as the band set up.

"Want something to drink while we wait?" Gabe asked after they found a good spot off to the side of the stage.

"I would love something. How about a lemonade from one of those spots we passed earlier?"

"Sounds great. Wait here, and I'll be right back."

While she waited, she took in the sights and sounds. She didn't go to Lafayette often, but always loved it when she visited. The people were friendly. They'd start talking to you in the line at the grocery store, and before long, they knew where you were from, where you were going, and who your family was. Several people had already nodded to her in greeting as she stood there waiting for Gabe to return.

She tapped her feet to the lively beat, unable to resist.

"Wanna dance, *cher?*" The guy standing in front of her appeared to be in his sixties, face leathery from sun. He wore a gimme hat from a local oilfield company. He was about a foot shorter than she was and absolutely precious.

Grace nodded and took his hand.

• • • •

"I HAVEN'T FELT THIS good in weeks," she said as she and Gabe took shelter in the shade of an old oak trees. Gabe spread out a blanket he had in his backpack and they took a seat. Her heart still beat fast, she could feel the flush in her cheeks, and her legs were almost shaky. The older guy had led her through the spirited first dance, and she had danced every dance until Geno stopped playing over an hour later. She jitterbugged, waltzed with Gabe, and two-stepped with others. She had tried to teach Gabe to jitterbug, but after both of them ended up doubled over in laughter, they had given up.

"I'm so glad," Gabe said as he reached for her hand.

"This was a great idea. Thank you, Gabe."

"You're so welcome," he said. Taking her hand, he pulled her closer. He leaned down and touched his lips to hers. It was a soft kiss at first, until Grace returned the kiss. The kiss soon turned more heated.

Grace was the first to break the contact. She leaned back and looked at him. "Can we just make today about you and me. Nothing about the past. Nothing about the future. Just today."

"Of course."

"I promise we will talk. Soon. But this feels good today. To be away. To be with you. Let's just enjoy that."

He smiled and leaned down and kissed her softly.

"Whatever you want, baby."

"What I want right now is some alligator on a stick! We need to re-energize if we're going to keep dancing."

"I got that. You wait right here. Relax. Today is all about you, baby."

• • • •

THE LAST BAND OF THE day wound down, and Grace and Gabe made their way through the crowd back to his bike.

"What do you want to do now?" he asked.

"I don't know. How about we check out some local music?"

"Sounds good. I talked to my roommate, Nate, who's from here and Emily earlier when I was making plans. They recommended downtown and it's only, like, ten minutes from here. How about we check that out?"

"Perfect."

As they drove the short distance from the park, Grace enjoyed the sights of the town. The University of Lafayette, the college Emily had gone to, was on the right. The oak trees that graced the campus were haloed in the golden glow of the dwindling light.

The weather was perfect, the night was warm and smelled of soil and fresh cut grass. Clean. Fresh. New. Perfect.

Gabe pulled into a parking spot when they arrived downtown. They secured their helmets, then took off on a stroll down the street that was lined with restaurants, bars, and art galleries. Hand in hand they walked, stopping here and there to window shop at the galleries.

As they passed bars, they would stop to listen for a moment. They stopped a couple of times before finally settling on a sound they liked. They went in and took seats at the bar.

Gabe ordered their drinks, then they swiveled in their stools to watch the band.

"I was talking to the bartender about the band. You know this band is my roommate's old band, right? Destination Sanity. He used to play bass for them before he moved to Austin to join our band," Gabe said.

"I like them. They have a cool vibe. And that lead singer is something else. I can tell. Listen to those jokes he's telling between songs."

"Right?' Gabe said.

"I like this place. It's so laid back. Look at everyone," Grace said. "It's so different than New Orleans."

"Austin isn't that much different."

Grace exhaled. "I can't go to Austin. Not yet."

"You don't have to do anything you do want to do."

Grace smiled and patted his thigh. "I may one day. But not yet."

He put his hand over hers. "Whenever you're ready."

"I still have some issues to work out. I still need my mornings with Noah, and I need to find my voice. I have to do this for me. I can't do a relationship right now."

He took her hand and raised it to his lips. "I understand, Grace. Do what you have to do for you. And know that I'm here for you."

"How about we wander down the street? Let's enjoy this town while we're here."

"You got it, *cher*," he said.

They finished their drinks and continued down the strip of bars on Jefferson Street. They stopped to look at the local art featured in the windows of the galleries. Colorful paintings in reds, purples, blues, and yellows that reflected the joy in which these people lived. Jewelry made from oyster shells or fired glass was featured in another window. The other establishments were bars or restaurants, and all had people spilling in and out of them.

When they heard another band that intrigued them, they stopped in.

"Bartender says the band playing is Leauxco," Gabe said after he ordered their drinks.

"So, we went from Destination Sanity to Leauxco?" Grace said, raising an eyebrow. "Is this a trend?'

"Maybe so," Gabe said. They continued drinking and listening to the band. Gabe's hand rested on her thigh.

Drinks in hand, they swayed in time to the music.

"If I can reach you, I'm gonna wanna touch you," sang the lead singer.

"Wanna dance?" Gabe asked.

"I do."

"If I touch you, I'm going to wanna kiss you."

Grace swayed along the music with Gabe, enjoying the feel of him next to her. She relaxed and enjoyed dancing with him. Her hand rested on his well-defined arm.

"He's right, you know," Gabe said.

"What you mean?"

"If I keep touching you, I'm going to want to kiss you," he said.

"Do it, then."

He stopped moving and looked down at her. "You sure?"

"I am."

Slowly, he lowered his head and brushed his lips against hers. The kiss was gentle at first, then became more urgent. He pulled her closer. Grace could feel his grin against her lips as her hands reached around his middle to pull him closer.

"How about we get out of here?" he asked after placing one last kiss on her lips.

"Where are we going to go?"

"Nate told me about some houseboat rentals on the swamp in a town called Henderson. I made a reservation."

"That sounds awesome. Lead the way."

Gabe took her hand, raised it to his lips, then pulled her close. He kissed her forehead. "Let's go." He clasped her hand in his and they walked out of the bar.

Chapter Twenty-Two

G abe enjoyed the feel of Grace close to him as they drove down I-10 to the Henderson exit. The drive was less than twenty minutes. They rolled to a stop in front of a small bar and convenience store that looked like it had been there for the last fifty years. In the dim light of the one streetlight, you could see the weathered wraparound deck that surrounded the small building. A boat dock and a few houseboats dotted the shore.

"Turtle's Bar," Grace said as they dismounted. "Sounds like Snapper's."

"It does," Gabe said. "Wanna go in and have a drink?"

"Maybe tomorrow. I'm exhausted. Can we just get a couple to go?"

"Of course. Wait here if you want, and I'll be back with drinks and a key."

"Sounds wonderful."

As Grace waited, she wandered the wraparound porch and out behind to the covered deck. Through the open window of the bar, she could hear the small crowd in the bar. Their voices mingled with the Lynyrd Skynyrd that played on the jukebox.

After dark, there wasn't much boat traffic at the dock, but there were a few lights on the houseboats. The smells of Cajun cooking and BBQ floated on the breeze. Stars dotted the dark night sky.

"You ready?" Gabe said as he walked up behind her. He wrapped his arms around her waist, hugging her close to him. When she leaned back into his embrace, he placed a light kiss on the top of her head.

"It's gorgeous here," Grace said.

"Yes, it is. The one to the far right is ours for the night. You wanna go check it out?"

"I do."

Hand in hand, they walked down the dock to the small houseboat that was anchored there. Gabe unlocked the door and let them in. The houseboat was quaint and cozy, in true Cajun camp fashion. It was open, only the bathroom was separated from the rest. No big city frills here, there was a small kitchenette and two beds covered in blue bedspreads. The walls were decorated with pictures of fishing, catching them, or bodies of water.

Gabe set their bags down on one of the beds, then crossed over to where Grace was standing. He took her hand. "Come see."

He led them through the door that led out to the back deck.

The swamp stretched out in front of them. The water slapping against the boat and the sounds of crickets and other night creatures were the only sounds. The old cypress trees were dark shadows in the moonlight.

"Gabe, it's perfect." She turned to face him, and as she did, he lifted her chin to meet his kiss. It was a slow, gentle exploration. As his hands circled her waist, her hands wound their way up his back. Tender at first, the kiss became more demanding. Her hands roamed his back. He tangled his hand in her hair.

Finally, breathless, he leaned back, smiling. "Damn."

She grinned back. "I agree."

He took her hand and led her to one of the lounge chairs. He sat back and pulled her down, to cradle her in his arms.

"We're going to need to talk eventually," Grace said.

"I know," he agreed. "But not tonight."

"You're leaving though."

"I am. But I told you, I'm coming back. You aren't getting rid of me that easily."

Grace tucked her head under his chin. When she rested her hand on his chest, he threaded his fingers with his. His other arm wrapped around her, holding her tight against him.

As she yawned, he kissed the top of her head. "Sleep Grace."

Closing her eyes, Grace smiled.

Chapter Twenty-Three

Grace was back on the beach, watching the flames devour those sheets. The air around her was as cold as the bottle of champagne in her hand.

In her other hand, she held pictures. Photos of her singing with Brent on stage. She took one last look at them and threw them on the fire too.

Grace watched the pictures curl up and melt away. Watched the sparks from the fire float up and away, disappearing into the dark night sky.

• • • •

GRACE TOOK HER NORMAL spot on the houseboat. She hadn't met with Noah the last few days. Not since her beach breakdown and her getaway with Gabe. But she needed it, her dreams were still haunting her, as evidenced by that morning's nightmare. Gabe and Ryder were still leaving. Their goodbye party was tonight in New Orleans. Grace wasn't going. As bad as she wanted to, she had the homecoming float to tend to that night. And it was New Orleans. Grace wasn't sure she was ready for that yet.

What a wonderful night and morning she had spent with Gabe. She had woken up as the sun came out, still in his arms. When she stirred, so had he. They had made coffee in the small kitchenette, then spent the rest of the day exploring the area. They had brunch at a wonderful place in Breaux Bridge that featured a Cajun band. Grace had danced and eaten more than she had in weeks.

They had taken the long way home, through the coastal towns of Morgan City and Houma, avoiding I-10 and the traffic on the basin bridge.

He had dropped her off at Joey's, and after a long, lingering goodbye kiss, had gone to his own house.

She heard Noah approach and waited for him to appear. Soon, he popped his head out through the sliding glass doors. Two mugs in hand.

"How did you know?"

"I just did."

"Yeah right. You probably just made two cups anyway."

Noah laughed. "Maybe so."

"You guys still going to New Orleans tonight?"

"Yeah. It was Carly's idea. I think she just wanted to go to New Orleans. The rest of us are going along for the ride."

"Should be fun."

"I think so."

"We're going to miss you in New Orleans," Noah said.

"I can't go, Noah. Not yet. And I have this homecoming thing."

"I know. You'll get there eventually."

They looked out at the horizon for a while, sipping their coffee. Finally, Grace asked the question that had been gnawing at her since she woke up.

"What do you think it means when your nightmares start changing. Mine are different now."

"I think it means that you're learning how to heal. It means you've stopped running."

"Do you think they'll ever completely go away?"

"No. But they'll eventually lessen in frequency. And you'll figure out what triggers them, and that will help. Important dates, something you see on TV, a memory, those things all mess with my head."

Grace took a sip of her coffee and considered his answer. He was right. Until that morning, she hadn't had a nightmare since her beach episode. She attributed it to exhaustion, but maybe it was the float tonight, the music, that triggered the dream.

She nodded and smiled, staring out at the rising sun. "You know, Noah, I think I'm going to be okay."

He reached out and placed his hand on hers. "Yes, you are. Now, one more cup of coffee?"

She held out her cup. "Yes, I need it.'

· · · ·

AT THE LOT WHERE THE homecoming floats were parked, Grace walked past the other classes' and organizations' floats and the convertibles that would carry the queen and the rest of the court in all their finery. Much to her students' amusement, Precious Mouton had not won her bid for queen, despite her "recruiting" efforts.

The students had done a great job. Grace never would have been able to do this on her own. She didn't have a decorative bone in her body. The bottom was covered in black vinyl. The students had cut out and painted flames that rose up from the base. Two huge guitars crossed in the middle, surrounded by more flames. *Rock On* was in neon letters on the banner. The students riding would all wear costumes from popular acts of the day like Vanilla Ice, Gun's N Roses, and Prince.

At the last minute, Grace had decided against the conservative slacks and shirt and pulled on the black skirt she had worn often on stage. She had pulled on her silver sequin tank, and huge silver hoops adorned her ears. She even teased her hair, just a little bit. She wasn't going too overboard.

She looked down at her outfit and the black high heeled boots. She played with the charm bracelet around her wrist.

Gabe, she thought as her fingers touched on the angel wings.

"Well, if it isn't our little songbird," came Officer Mouton's grating voice from behind her. "This theme seems to fit you."

"What are you doing here?" Grace asked as she turned to face him.

"It's my job to check all the floats for safety before letting the kids ride them. Especially your little band of rebels. I'll be checking this float for contraband."

Grace stiffened. He was not going to insult her kids. "Leave my kids out of this and get on with your job. Go on," she said when she saw his eyes lingering on her for just a little too long.

"Nice outfit," he said. "Did you wear that on stage with Brent? He still talks about you. He tells me things. And I've heard our little songbird has lost her voice."

Grace looked down at the bracelet again, she smiled at Noah's Semper Fi charm.

"I really don't give a damn. About Brent, or even you. Why should I care what some small-town bully with a badge talks about? You can kiss my ass if you think I spend one moment even thinking about you. Much less talking about you. I have better things to do."

"Ms. Delchamp! Get 'em!"

Shit, the students. Grace turned to see a group of them standing behind her.

To hide her embarrassment, she took a big bow with a flourish of her hand. The students clapped then got busy exclaiming over each other and their costumes. They took pictures of each other, some took pictures with her.

As the students filed in, so did parents, many exclaiming over the float. Some stopped by Grace to tell her how good everything looked.

"Great job," one parent told her.

"Thank you," Grace said.

"Ms. Delchamp. Are you aware that we have a strict faculty dress code? I would never get away with wearing a skirt like that."

Grace slowly turned her head toward the speaker, eyebrows raised at the catty tone.

"Excuse me?" she asked, not surprised to see the Ms. Benoit and her husband standing there. Mary's eyes were wide with saccharine sweetness.

"I just meant, I could *never* wear a skirt like that."

Grace cut her eyes sideways again.

Mary started to open her mouth again. "Don't get me wrong—"

Grace snapped.

"Oh, I got you all right," Grace said. "Maybe if you would wear a skirt like this every now and then, your husband wouldn't be looking at me like he wants to see what's up mine."

Mary's eyes widened as she inhaled a deep breath. "Well, I never."

"That's right. You never! But maybe you should. Life is about living and enjoying it." As soon as the words came out, Grace knew she was done with this job. At this point, if she was going down, she was going down in the proverbial flames. She was done with hiding. She was going to live again.

"Guess what?" she asked loud enough for the kids milling around to hear. "Looks like your Ms. Delchamp *will* be performing on this float. Let's load up, kids. It's time."

She hiked her skirt up a wee bit more and went to the DJ stand manned by Mr. Benoit.

"I'll take that mic," she said.

While he readied the music and the float began to roll, Grace took the red lipstick she often wore on stage out of her bag and applied it. She added a dash of lip gloss and teased her hair a bit more for good measure.

When the first song began to play, Grace felt a flash of fear. She nodded her head in time with the introduction. Then, when it was time for the vocals, without hesitation, Grace began to sing.

The kids went wild. Two even jumped up to be back-up singers. Grace handed them a mic. Phones came out as students started snapping pics. Grace smiled as members of the faculty and some parents glared at her from the crowd. She winked at Ms. Benoit, who had taken a sullen seat beside her husband.

Grace finished the parade and handed the mic over to one of the students standing behind her. After a few more pics and hugs, she smiled, waved, and walked away. She was going to New Orleans. She was going to go find Gabe.

Chapter Twenty-Five

Grace ducked into the popular French Quarter bar. It was a Friday night, and the place was already close to full. She made her way through the crowd, past the worn mechanical bull that some drunken tourist was about to take a turn on. Carly and crew were stationed by the DJ station, the front of an old red car. The DJ was positioned behind the windshield. Another guy walked through the crowd with a mic, walking out of the bar and onto Bourbon Street to entice customers inside, occasionally holding the mic out for customers to sing along with the song.

Carly, Joey, Emily, Noah, Kevin, and Gabe were nestled in the corner. Ryder was leaning against the railing of the bull riding area. He had a beer in one hand, his long, lanky form bent down, one leg resting on the bottom railing. Grace grinned, knowing he was smiling. Later, she was sure, he'd have his try at the bull, after a few people had been thrown. He would wait until he had a full audience, preferably full of good-looking women.

She walked up behind him and placed her hand on his back. He turned slowly, and seeing her, he rewarded her with one of his smiles.

"I thought you had that parade thing?" he said.

Grace laughed, and he smiled back. He leaned down and kissed her forehead.

"It's been too long since I heard that," he said.

"It's a long story. I'll tell you later."

"You bet your sweet ass you will."

He lit a cigarette and took a long drag, looking her up and down. Satisfied that all was finally well with her, he winked. "Gonna join me on that dance floor later?"

"You bet. We got to show these tourists how it's done."

"You're damn right."

"Let me go say hello to the others," she said. "To Gabe."

He gave her another quick peck on the forehead. "Good deal. Try to talk Carly out of that fool idea to ride that damn bull."

Grace laughed. "Yeah right. I'll just get my camera ready."

Carly's eyes widened in surprise as she saw Grace walk up. "Grace, what are you doing here?"

Grace smiled at Carly, but her eyes never left Gabe's. Her heart beat faster as she saw his face light up when he spotted her.

"It's a long story," she said.

Carly pulled a stool up and patted it. "Have a seat. I wanna hear all about it."

She sat next to Gabe, whose hand immediately reached for hers. He leaned in close to whisper in her ear, "I'm so glad you came."

"Not right now, but soon," she said to Carly. Then whispered back to Gabe, "Me too." She squeezed his hand.

"Okay. Wanna shot?"

"Why not? We're celebrating tonight."

"Celebrating? Is there something else you aren't telling me?" Carly asked, raising a brow.

"I'll tell you later. I thought you were getting those shots?"

"Right. I need that liquid courage anyway. I'm gonna ride that bull later."

Grace just shook her head. Once Carly got an idea in her head, it was almost impossible to change her mind.

Carly left to order the round of shots, and Grace greeted the rest of the group. Instead of returning to the stool Carly had pulled out, Grace went to stand beside Noah, who was there with Kevin, leaning her back against the bar like he did. Never would Noah have his back to a room. He always had to see what was going on.

"You're leaving, aren't you?" he asked, taking a sip of his beer.

She nodded. "I am."

"With Gabe?"

"Yes."

He nodded and smiled. "Good. You telling the others?"

"Not yet, but soon. I probably should tell Gabe first."

Noah laughed, then said, "Yeah, probably so."

"You going to talk your sister out of riding that bull?"

"Of course not. I'm smarter than that."

After greeting Kevin, she asked him, "Are you thinking about running against Jacque Mouton in the next election?"

He nodded.

"Good," Grace said. "If you do, I've got some information for you. It's time those Moutons paid for their actions." Grace was going to sing like a bird on Brent and Denis Mouton.

"I agree."

Carly's voice rose, and they looked over to see Carly and Joey's argument had obviously grown more heated. Joey's stance was tight, his features rigid. Grace shook her head on that one. She'd already tried to push the two together to no good result. It was up to the two of them to find their own way.

She rejoined Gabe at the bar. She sipped the drink he pressed into her hand, and looked at these people who had meant so much to her the last few months. For all her life really. If she didn't have them, who knew where she'd be right now.

A spirited country song started playing, and Ryder was by her side, hand extended. She took it with a smile, and he led her to the dance floor.

The song was a fast one, as were their steps and twirls. Grace followed Ryder's complicated shuffling steps to the beat, the quick twists and turns leaving her half dizzy, breathless, and feeling more alive than she had since the festival in Lafayette.

Soon, the two had attracted the attention of the bar and the DJ.

"Ladies and gentlemen, we have some real dancers on the dance floor. Check them out."

The crowd in the bar formed a semicircle between the dance floor and the mechanical bull area. Some clapped along with the beat, and some hooted in appreciation.

Grace's smile widened when she heard Carly's whistle over the sound of the crowd and the music.

The song ended. Grace and Ryder turned to the crowd, giving a breathless half bow. Grace walked back to the group at the bar, knowing Ryder would want to stay behind and talk to his new groupies.

As Grace walked up, Carly was doing a shot. She slammed down the plastic glass on the wooden bar. "It's settled. I'm doing it."

Joey shook his head and sighed. "Fine. Find Ryder. That's his arena."

Grace's lips twitched at the pun she knew Joey was unaware he'd made.

Carly walked over to Ryder and talked to him for a moment. He shoved his black cowboy hat onto her head. Apparently, she needed a cowboy hat to ride the bull. Ryder shook his head and lit a cigarette. Grace ordered a beer and another drink and joined him at the railing. Carly paid the five dollars for the ride and walked over to the guy in charge. Grace watched as he gave her some pointers and helped her onto the bull.

Carly smiled and winked at the crowd that gathered around her. She tucked one wrist under the roping and put one hand on Ryder's cowboy hat.

"Ladies and gentlemen, we have a rider!" The DJ said, and more people gathered around to watch.

The bull started moving, slowly at first, and Carly held her own, moving in time with the computerized animal. It didn't last long though, the operator toggled the controls and the bull moved faster. Grace saw Carly's eyes widen as the bull moved faster and faster. Grace looked at Joey, whose face was a stony mask. Grace believed he would've turned away if he could, but he had to see. Had to be sure Carly wasn't hurt.

The bull moved up and down faster, and Grace could see Carly was having a hard time holding on. Grace grabbed Ryder's arm.

He looked down at her and laughed. "She's going to fall and it will hurt. But it's going to hurt her pride worse than anything."

And seconds later, Carly was thrown from the bull onto the black cushioned floor.

"At least she has cushions," Ryder said. "I fall on the ground. That shit hurts."

Ryder downed the rest of his beer and dropped it down onto the bar. "I'll get her. Joey may kill her."

Grace joined her brother at the bar, who had turned his back on the bull riding, probably after seeing Ryder go take care of Carly. Grace put her hand on Joey's back.

"She's okay, yeah."

"She's an idiot," he said.

"Carly is Carly, "Grace said.

"She's still an idiot."

"Sometimes, yes," Grace said, "but aren't we all sometimes?"

Joey turned his brown eyes on her. "What do you mean?"

"Exactly what I said. You are one of the biggest sometimes."

"I don't know what you're talking about."

"You know exactly what I'm talking about."

He looked away.

"Keep looking away," Grace said. "A wise friend of mine said you can't keep running away from the truth."

Joey took a long sip of his beer but still didn't look at her. "I'm not running from anything."

Grace blew out an exasperated sigh. "Fine then, brother. Keep believing that."

"You're one to talk, you know? You're letting Gabe walk away."

"Don't turn this on me, no. I'm leaving with Gabe."

He looked at her then, smiling. "Is that right?"

"Yep."

"Does he know?"

"Nope."

He laughed. "Well, you'll have to keep me posted."

"Only if you promise me to make your own move."

His face clouded over. "What if I lose her?"

"What if you don't?"

He reached over and ruffled her hair, and she frowned. "I'm not twelve anymore, you know."

"I see that."

"Okay, then. How about we head on down to Cat's Meow? I'm in the mood for some karaoke."

Joey's eyes widened again. "You're singing again?"

She smiled. "I am."

He hugged her close to his side and got Em and Noah's attention. He leaned in close so they could hear him over the noise and talked for a moment. Em smiled at her, and Noah winked. Ryder joined them then with a limping Carly. Joey said a quick word to Ryder, and Ryder smiled, and together they all left the bar.

Grace stopped when heard the '80s music blaring. Brent and the band were playing. She heard his voice blasting out *Pour Some Sugar on Me*. It was a song that she used to sing. She waited for the nausea to hit. She smiled when it didn't. She nodded to the rest, and motioned them to the door. Ryder's face clouded when he saw where they were going, but she raised an eyebrow and smiled. They ordered drinks and turned to watch the band. Brent was definitely working it tonight. His blond hair was long and hanging down his Pink Floyd t-shirt. He had handkerchiefs streaming down his microphone pole. He leaned down with the pole into the crowd.

Grace shook her head. That band would never be more than they were right then. Always playing other people's songs in a tourist trap where people paid seven dollars for a three-dollar beer. She was done with it. Done with it all.

Brent noticed her then. He straightened, jutted his pelvis forward, and smiled.

What a joke. Grace threw back her head and laughed. Then laughed again when his eyes widened, then narrowed. Grace downed the rest of her drink and nodded her head toward the stage. It was a challenge she knew he couldn't resist.

He wrapped up the Def Leppard song and turned to speak with the band for a moment. The older members of the band, friends of hers who she hadn't talked to since she left, smiled when they saw her in the audience.

"Well, folks," Brent said to the crowd, "looks like we have a visitor tonight. New Orleans, give a warm welcome to one of our former bandmates, Grace Delchamp."

Grace hopped on the stage and took a mic from the bassist. She turned to the band to give them a song title. They played the opening chords. Grace palmed the mic and gave the audience one of her signature smiles. In the light, she could see Gabe wink, and she nodded.

"Ladies and gentlemen, it feels good to be back up here on stage. And to have all my friends here with me."

She pointed them out. "Give these peeps a round of applause. They are truly some awesome people. In fact, I'm dedicating this song to them. It's about bad days, friends, and sticking together. You may have heard it, it goes like this."

"Here's to us," Grace sang, beaming when Carly raised her glass.

Grace worked the crowd just like old times, and soon she had the crowd singing along and raising their own glasses.

She leaned down once to take the shot Carly brought her. Still singing, she looked Brent in the eye. "If they do you wrong, tell 'em to go to hell."

She downed the shot and threw the plastic cup out into the crowd.

The crowd went wild. Grace finished out the song and handed the mic to Brent.

"Touché," he said. "You know, you could stay and finish out the set."

"Go to hell," she said, and walked to meet Gabe, who was still smiling and clapping when she reached him.

He opened his arms, and she threw herself into his embrace. He leaned down and gave her a kiss that rivaled the high she got from performing.

He leaned back. "You looked good up there."

"I felt good. You ready to get outta here?"

"You betcha."

He threw an arm over her shoulder and said, "Let's go kick some karaoke ass at the Cat's Meow."

. . . .

GRACE AND GABE STROLLED down the boulevard, hand in hand. The sun was rising over the city's skyline. The rest of the group had retired to their rooms earlier. Grace and Gabe had chosen to enjoy a leisurely breakfast at one of the many diners still open.

Gabe pulled her into the lobby of a hotel.

"What are you doing?" Grace asked.

"I want you all to myself right now. And I shared a room with Joey and Ryder. Do you really want those around right now? You okay with that?"

Grace nodded.

Gabe paid for the room, and took her hand, leading her toward the elevator. As the doors swished closed, he pulled her into his arms, and lowered his lips to hers. "Tonight, it's just about you and me."

She smiled. "You mean today?"

He laughed. "I guess you're right."

The elevator swished open again, and he led them to their room. He keyed it open. Grace crossed to the window and opened the curtain that revealed a view of the New Orleans skyline. She smiled as Gabe came up behind her. He wrapped his arms around her, his lips nuzzling her neck.

"I'm tired of running. I'm tired of running from the truth." She took another sip of her drink then looked up into his eyes. "I'm tired of running from you. This isn't going to be easy, you know. I still have issues to work out."

"I'm here for you, Grace. I told you already. It's not just you. It's we. We'll work this out."

He reached out a hand and cupped her cheek, his eyes piercing hers again., He leaned in closer, and placed a soft kiss on her lips. His hand came up to cradle her neck. Grace's arms reached around his waist, an open invitation.

An invitation he took as he led them to the bed.

Epilogue

New Year's Eve

Grace and Gabe walked into Snapper's. Carly's eyes lit up as she saw the two come in. She hurried from behind the bar to come envelope them in hugs.

"Glinda told me you guys were coming in today! I'm so excited! Have a seat. I'll get you some drinks started! Have you eaten? Joey's back there cooking if you want something? Joey! Grace and Gabe are here!"

Joey came in the bar through the swinging wooden doors that separated the bar from the kitchen area. "Grace!" He, too, came around from behind the bar to shake Gabe's hand, then he hugged Grace close. He left his hands on her arms so he could take a good look at her. Seeing her happy, the anger in her face gone, he smiled and hugged her close again.

"Austin's been good to you," Carly said.

Grace smiled and looked at Gabe. "Yes, yes, it has."

"Did you text Ryder? What about Em and Noah?"

"They're all coming. We stopped in at Glinda's already to freshen up. We texted them right before we ate. So, no, we aren't hungry," Grace said.

Emily and Noah were the first to arrive. Then Ryder. Soon they were all gathered around the corner of the bar. The guys were playing pool, Carly, who had ended her day shift, had taken charge of playing the jukebox. It was all like old times.

Cheech, as they all called him, approached the girls who sat in the corner, surrounded by whichever guys weren't playing pool at the moment. Always the protective barrier.

"Hey, ladies," he said. "Wanna hear some music?"

"Would love to," Carly said, "but I have an idea. Why don't we get Gabe and Grace to play a few? Would you guys do that? We'd love to hear y'all play."

Gabe glanced at Grace, who nodded.

"I'll go get the guitars," said Gabe.

"I'll hook up the sound system," said Grace.

"I have a request," Emily said.

"What's that?" Grace said.

She smiled at Cheech and at Noah. "How about I'll be home for Christmas?

Noah laughed. "At least it's closer to Christmas this time."

"Sure thing," Grace said.

Gabe stepped out to get the guitars and gear. Ryder set down his pool cue and came over to her.

"You look good, Grace," he said.

"I feel good," she said.

He leaned down and kissed her on the cheek. He took his black cowboy hat off and shoved it on her head. "Good."

She leaned in and rested her head on his chest for a moment. Then looked up at him. "Thank you," she said.

"No thanks necessary. Now, get that ass up there and sing. We've missed that voice."

Grace and Gabe made quick work of the equipment and soon were sitting on the makeshift stage of Snapper's.

"First up, we're going to play an original song that Gabe and I have been working on. You guys are going to be the first to hear it," Grace said into the mic. She motioned to Gabe, and he began to play.

After a few chords from Gabe's guitar, Grace began to sing, "Deepest are the wounds without a scar at all."

It was a slow song. Emily grabbed Noah and they headed to the area in front of the band that was used as a dance floor. Carly grabbed Joey. And Ryder, not to be left out, found Allison.

Grace's eyes met Gabe's, and she smiled.

They played until 11:59, then led the countdown to midnight. Carly had made sure everyone had champagne as the countdown finished.

"Five, four, three, two, one!" Gabe leaned into kiss her softly. "Happy New Year baby."

"Happy New...what the hell?" Grace exclaimed.

Gabe turned to see what she was looking at. His eyes widened too. Joey and Carly were wrapped in each other's arms, still kissing after the countdown.

Ryder appeared beside Grace and Gabriel. He wrapped an arm around Grace's shoulder and nodded to the two still embracing by the bar.

He said in his low, Southern drawl, "Well, it's about damn time."

Read More

Will a hurricane's aftermath lead Carly to her happily-ever-after, once and for all?
Amazon Buy Link: https://amzn.to/35JaVYz

"Saving Grace"

Rescued in a New Orleans alley, Furby has been Grace's comfort and constant companion. After he is injured, his fearless personality and determination encourages Grace to let go of the past and embrace the future.

Amazon Buy Link: https://amzn.to/3mOrWG4

About the Author

A.L. Vincent is a teacher/writer who lives in the heart of Cajun Country. Born in Oklahoma, Vincent became fascinated with South Louisiana after reading Interview With the Vampire. Finally, she became a Cajun transplant in 2001. When not getting lost in a story line, Vincent can be found cooking or enjoying live local music.

Subscribe to my newsletter for all the updates!
http://eepurl.com/bRiinr

Don't miss out!

Visit the website below and you can sign up to receive emails whenever A. L. Vincent publishes a new book. There's no charge and no obligation.

https://books2read.com/r/B-A-FJAK-FWLNB

BOOKS 2 READ

Connecting independent readers to independent writers.

Also by A. L. Vincent

Bon Chance Boonies
Running on Empty